By Gary Paulsen

PUBLISHED BY FARRAR STRAUS GIROUX

Gone to the Woods: Surviving a Lost Childhood

How to Train Your Dad

Northwind

WIND

GARY PAULSEN

FARRAR STRAUS GIROUX
NEW YORK

Farrar Straus Giroux Books for Young Readers

An imprint of Macmillan Publishing Group, LLC

120 Broadway, New York, NY 10271 • mackids.com

Our books may be purchased in bulk for promotional, educational, or business
use. Please contact your local bookseller or the Macmillan Corporate and
Premium Sales Department at (800) 221-7945 ext. 5442 or by email at
MacmillanSpecialMarkets@macmillan.com.

Library of Congress Cataloging-in-Publication Data

Names: Paulsen, Gary, author.

Title: Northwind / Gary Paulsen,

Description: First edition. | New York : Farrar Straus Giroux Books for
    Young Readers, 2022. | Audience: Grades 4–6. | Summary: When sickness
    decimates his fishing camp, an orphan named Leif flees north in a cedar
    canoe, journeying along a brutal but beautiful coastline.

Identifiers: LCCN 2021027784 | ISBN 9780374314200 (hardcover)

Subjects: CYAC: Wilderness survival—Fiction. | Survival—Fiction. |
    Orphans—Fiction. | LCGFT: Novels.

Classification: LCC PZ7.P2843 Nm 2022 | DDC [Fic]—dc23

LC record available at https://lccn.loc.gov/2021027784

First edition, 2022

Book design by Trisha Previte

Printed in the United States of America by Lakeside Book Company,
Harrisonburg, Virginia

ISBN 978-0-374-31420-0 (hardcover)

10 9 8 7 6 5 4 3 2 1

This book is dedicated to Jennifer Flannery,
my agent of thirty years. She has been, more than once,
the what, where, when, and how of my work.

Contents

The Saga of Sea Child

AND IT CAME TO PASS HE WAS BORNE OF A
WOMAN OF THE SEA,
BORNE OF A SEA WOMAN, WITH A BLOOD
CLOT HELD TIGHTLY
    IN HIS TINY FIST.
A SIGN.
A SIGN TO TELL, TO TELL OF HARDSHIP AND
DANGER IN THE LIFE TO COME,
    TO COME, FROM THE TINY FIST AND CLOT.
AND THE MOTHER, OF NO REMEMBERED NAME,
DID DIE BIRTHING THE BOY
    AND THE FATHER, ALSO OF NO
    REMEMBERED NAME,

HAD PASSED TO VALHALLA FIGHTING A
    WHALE.
AND AS THERE WAS NO OTHER NAMED FAMILY
    THE BOY WAS BORN AN ORPHAN.
ALONE.
    TO LIVE ALONE ON THE DOCKS, A DOCK
    BOY, A WHARF BOY, NURSED BY SUCKING
    RAGS DIPPED IN SOUR GOAT'S MILK AND
    FISH OIL,
    FED ON SCRAPS OTHERS WOULD CHEW TO
    SOFTEN,
    DRESSED IN YET MORE RAGS WITH CRUDELY
    CARVED WOODEN SHOES,
    ALWAYS HALF NAKED.
HE WAS THAT BOY.
THAT BOY.
AND THEY CALLED HIM THE WHARF RAT AND
NAMED HIM LEIF
    FOR NO OTHER PERSON ON THOSE DOCKS
    HAD THAT NAME.
AND WHEN HE WAS OLD ENOUGH TO WALK

THEY TOOK HIM ON THE BOATS.
FOR ALL HIS YOUNG LIFE HE WAS PASSED FROM
ONE BOAT TO THE NEXT, TO THE NEXT, TO
THE NEXT.
NO LONGER THE WHARF RAT NAMED LEIF BUT
A BOAT RAT NAMED LEIF.
AND WHEN HE COULD USE HIS HANDS THEY SET
HIM TO REPAIRING NETS,
    SEWING RIPPED NETS, TORN CLOTHING, AND
    SHARPENING THE SEAL-KILLING HARPOONS,
    BEATING HIM WITH WOODEN RODS IF HE DID
    THEM WRONG.
AND THEY MADE HIM COOK GREASY EEL MEAT
THAT THE SAILORS WOULD EAT,
    CLAIMING IT WAS SOFT AND WOULD BE
    EASY TO PUKE WHEN THEY BECAME SEASICK.
ACROSS ONE OCEAN, INTO ANOTHER OCEAN,
THEN NORTH LOOKING NOT FOR WHALES—
    WHICH WERE TOO HARD TO KILL—BUT FOR
    SEALS, FOR THEIR GREASE-MEAT AND FURS.
ALWAYS AFTER FURS.

FOR SEAL FURS SHINED LIKE GOLD PIECES.
ALWAYS NORTH, WHERE THE SEAL FUR WAS
THICKEST AND MADE FOR BETTER WARMTH.
AND THE BOY GREW AND WAS FIVE SUMMERS,
THEN SIX, THEN EIGHT, AND TEN,
    AND TWELVE SUMMERS, TAKEN ON ONE
    BOAT, THEN ANOTHER AND ANOTHER,
    UNTIL WHEN HE SLEPT IN HIS DREAM STORY
    IT SEEMED LIKE ALL ONE OCEAN,
    AND WHEN HE CAME AWAKE IT STILL SEEMED
    LIKE ONE OCEAN JUST AS ALL BOATS
    SEEMED LIKE ONE BOAT AND ALL EEL
    MEAT—WHICH HE LEARNED TO PUKE—
    SEEMED LIKE ONE MEAT AND ALL PUKE
    SEEMED LIKE ONE PUKE
    AND ALL BEATINGS SEEMED LIKE ONE
    BEATING.
AND WINTERS.
THE BOY HAD WINTERS WHERE THE FREEZING
SEA BOILED IN BLOWN RAGE AND WAS
SOMETIMES SO COLD,

MEN'S FINGERS WOULD FREEZE BLACK AND
HAVE TO BE CUT OFF,
AND THE BOY WOULD RUB OIL ON THEM
TO TOUGHEN THE STUBS,
AMAZED THAT MEN COULD STILL WORK
WITH ALMOST NO FINGERS.
NORTH.
FOR THE BETTER FURS THAT SHINED LIKE
GOLD.
UNTIL THEY WERE NORTH, HAD COME IN THIS
BOAT NORTH TO TURN EAST
IN THE GIANT STRAITS AND UP INTO THE
FORESTED WILDNESS
AND AN ISOLATED FISH CAMP WAS SET UP
WHERE A SMALL RIVER CAME INTO THE
SEA.
WHERE THE SHIP LEFT LEIF.
AND FOUR USED-UP AND PART-CRIPPLED OLD
MEN—ONE NAMED OLD CARL—AND A
SMALL THRALL BOY BOUGHT OFF A
WHALING SHIP ON WHICH A TRAVELING

WHARF WOMAN HAD BORNE THE CHILD
AND PASSED AND AFTER SHE WAS BURIED
AT SEA THE CREW FED THE SMALL BOY ON
FISH SAUCE AND SEAL MILK CUT FROM DEAD
SEALS THAT HAD BEEN NURSING UNTIL HE
LEARNED TO WALK. BUT WITH THE WOMAN
GONE, THEY WANTED NO CHILDREN AND SO
SOLD HIM FOR A FOLDED BOLT OF HEAVY
SAILCLOTH.
AND HE WAS NAMED LITTLE CARL FOR HE HAD
NO OTHER NAME.
AND IN THIS FISH CAMP THEY WERE TO TAKE
SALMON FROM THE MOUTH OF THE RIVER AND
    SMOKE THE MEAT WHILE THE SHIP WAS
    GONE UP NORTH OUTSIDE THE GIANT
    ISLAND LOOKING FOR SEALS.
FOR THE SEALS WERE LIKE GOLD IN THE SUN.
AND THIS THEY DID, TAKING AND CUTTING
HUNDREDS OF SILVER SALMON AND
    SMOKING THEIR MEAT IN HAND-FASHIONED
    RACKS FOR DAYS UPON DAYS UNTIL THEY

HAD ENOUGH SMOKED AND DRIED FISH TO
LAST A WHOLE CREW OF A SHIP FOR AT
LEAST SIX MOONS.
AND THEY WAITED FOR DAYS UPON DAYS
AND THE SHIP DID NOT RETURN FOR THEM.
WOULD NEVER RETURN FOR THEM.
FOR THIS WAS A BAD COAST WITH TERRIBLE
RIPPING TIDES AND UNPREDICTABLE WINDS AND
ROCKY POINTS WHERE DEATH WAS ALWAYS
WAITING, AND THIS THEY KNEW AND SO
CAME TO KNOW THERE WOULD BE NO SHIP
COMING BACK FOR THEM AND THAT THE
SHIP AND CREW WERE GONE TO VALHALLA.
AND THEY WERE ALONE.
AND THEY WOULD HAVE TO LEAVE THIS PLACE
BY WAY OF THE SEA. THEY HAD A SMALL
CANOE, WHICH THEY HAD USED AXES TO
CARVE FROM A CEDAR LOG, FOR WORKING
IN THE STREAM SPEARING SALMON, BUT
THEY WERE TOO MANY FOR SO SMALL A
CRAFT AND IT WAS DECIDED THEY SHOULD

MAKE A LARGE DUGOUT CANOE TO TAKE
THEM ALL AND HAD CUT DOWN A GIANT
TREE TO ROLL-DRAG INTO CAMP.
AND THEY WOULD HAVE DONE THIS.
COULD HAVE DONE THIS.
EXCEPT DEATH FOUND THEM.

Men Who Have Lost Their Shadows

Nobody knew exactly when the dark ship came and to be sure at first they could not see it at all but only understood it was there in the thick fog by the smell.

There was a drifting stink of death.

A green-dark stench of burned and rotting greasy death came out of the fog, up the rocky bank, over the cedar canoe, into the small bark shelter huts they had made, past and around and through everything, slithering into every nook until all the men who had been deep in safe sleep came awake with the smell clawing into their every breath.

Death smell.

Death smell from a large wooden ship that rode heavy with the wind on dirty sails, hanging now in sloppy, stained loop-folds, coming from and with and in the fog so the dark and ugly ship seemed almost an extension of the fog itself.

There was no wind. Not a breath of it. And yet the boat moved, had moved along and down channels from the open sea, coming in silence—dead silence—on the moon-currents as the wild tides changed and pulled and pushed the silent drifting wooden ship until at last it came into the cove in front of the camp, seemingly of its own volition.

And stopped. Meant but not meant, not planned to be there but there, sending its death stink, the stink from blood-soaked decks and rotted gore and rendered fat, boiled off small whales, seals, dolphins—anything alive that had fat on it and could be made dead and the fat cooked out—ahead of the ship like a silent, dirty scream of filth.

But something else, too: the smell of dying, rotting men.

For a time there was a silence. Non-sound. A complete cessation of sound. Not even a croak from the crows and ravens circling above the drying racks. Night moved away and light came and the fog dissipated slowly, streaking around and away in gray swirls until the source of the stink could be seen, sitting in the cove, squat, thick-heavy in the water, its bow nudging against the rocky pebbles of the shore. A silent horror.

Then came the men.

They were not clean.

As crude and dirty and stinking as the ship, four men lowered a small workboat from the side of the ship and climbed down into it. One man used two oars to push the boat to the pebble beach, and three climbed out with great effort while the fourth held the small boat against the shore.

Some in the camp later said of the men that they seemed to be made from scraps of parts of the ship. Indescribably dirty, as worn as old wood, with their skin hanging from their bones, eyes red and deep in their sockets, and when they opened their mouths to smile a greeting, it could be seen that many teeth were gone.

They were in some strange way not unkind—though their appearance was in itself offensive—but so weak they could hardly stand. It was not even clear what they wanted, as their language made no sense. One of the elders said later it was as if their tongues tripped in some manner on their sparse teeth so the words rattled and could not be understood.

"Nyet," one said, shaking his head while he stuttered more unknown words, waving generally in the direction of the sea.

"Da," another added, nodding, pointing away from the sea and toward the shore, toward some thing up on the shore near the forest, the sailor waving and pointing, so that men in the camp out of politeness all looked up in the same direction as intently as they could, but saw nothing.

No part of the encounter was any better, made any sense. The weak men stood, weaving slightly, and the men in camp stood watching them and all was in silence, all in the tendrils of fog that still rolled back and forth. Real but not real, there but not there, men but not men.

Then the moon-currents came once more into the cove and captured the ship and it started to drift out of the cove and the boatmen hurried as best they could, staggering and nearly falling, and went back onto the vanishing ship.

Into the fog, into nothing. As if it had never been there, never been seen or heard or even smelled.

Gone.

Never seen again.

"They were spirit men," said one man from the camp, and who was to argue with him?

"Fog spirits—ghost men from the dark world . . ."

And those who said such things looked away in quiet fear at where the ship had been, and they shivered as if a dark-cold wind had come upon them.

A dead wind.

Death wind.

"They are men who have lost their shadows," said Old Carl, the eldest of the crew. "They are men who have done some great wrong and have lost their shadows." He waved his hand to the sky places. "They must search for their shadows to become men again. Whole men. They must drift forever in the death ship. And because they will never find their shadows again . . ."

He did not finish as he did not need to finish.

But the boy Leif wanted, needed, to know more and did not know how not to be rude, so he asked: "What happens because they cannot find their shadows?"

"They will bring misery," Old Carl said. "Misery. They will kill all joy and only bring misery with their foulness."

And because Old Carl was thought to be wise, everyone believed he was right. Even though they would never see the death ship again and the fish smoke fires drove away the smell of the ship and the man-dead stink, even then they knew something bad had to come. Had to come.

Something from the dark places would come in like the fog.

Something bad.

And eight days after the dark ship and men without shadows had gone the first men grew sick.

Two men first.

They became uncomfortably warm and then hot with a burning fever and so weak they could not stand and finally crawled into their huts to lie, still and sweating. Until vomit took them and they could not hold food or hot fish soup, the other men tried to feed them, and then not even water, and the vomit turned to blood and the second day even with what care they could be given the ghosts left the bodies of the two men almost at the same moment and they died.

Died.

Then the man who cared for them was hunted and found by the fever and went down and lost his ghost and likewise died.

Three of them.

But it did not end.

Instead the sickness became like a fire roaring through the camp and soon Old Carl started to burn.

Before he vomited blood, the old man took Leif and Little Carl and put them in the cedar canoe with some food and supplies, and sent them away.

"Go north," he said, pushing them as hard as he could from the shore. "The men without shadows made the air here sick with their poison. Head north where the air is not sick and where the water channels are so small they will not let the death ships pass. Keep going north and never come back. Never come back to this place. Never."

Yet Leif, who did not understand about not being rude, said: "But what of you? Can you not come?" For he liked, loved Old Carl in his fashion and if he found truth in himself he admitted that he felt fear, deep fear, in going off from the camp, into what wildness he did not know.

"All who are here will pass over the bridge. I am already sick. The fever has not taken you and Little Carl and you must leave. Now. Go away from this bad air, this bad dead place and do not look back, do not come back, do not even think back. Go."

And Old Carl turned away from the shore and walked back into the camp and the boy would always remember that he walked straight and tall though he was walking to his end, to his journey over the bridge of life into the other. The Other. Valhalla.

Then the canoe caught the moon-currents, which had turned and were heading out, and moved by itself around a point of forest that stuck out and Leif could not see the cove nor the camp any longer.

Since the current was heading north in the channel that passed the cove, Leif took up a paddle and dug it deep into the water next to the side of the cedar canoe and it slid forward. He neither cried nor choked a sound at his fear and sadness because Little Carl was watching him and one should not cry nor show fear in the face of small children.

It was early in the day when Old Carl pushed them off and the sun came up to warm their bare backs and Leif kept paddling hard, as if the mere act of hard work would ease the misery and pain and homesickness that worked at him.

Little Carl was very young and when it became obvious that he could not work at using the second paddle, he ate a small strip of smoked fish and curled up against the bundle of supplies and went to sleep.

Leif kept stroking with his paddle and the

canoe seemed to almost fly along with the moon-currents, but he kept digging the paddle deep even after his shoulders started to ache and his arms felt like they belonged to some other person.

All that day. They stopped once at a tiny stream that came falling out of the rocky edge of the forest, sitting in the canoe, and drank the water that they dipped with their hands, sweet and cold, and then Leif went back to paddling.

Heading north. Always north up through the wide channel all the afternoon and when the sun had moved over to shine on their shoulders Leif pulled into a narrow cove and used the braided rope to tie off the canoe to a small tree. He decided they would sleep in the canoe. What night came was exceedingly short this time of the year, and he was so tired he didn't feel like trying to start a fire.

Still sleep did not come easily. Little Carl was restless and though he didn't speak he kept coming to the edge of crying and would turn away without speaking. Leif touched the small boy's answer. He stared at Leif as if seeing through him. He would not eat and his forehead felt definitely warmer now, and Leif knew he was sick but didn't know what he could do about it. He splashed some cold seawater on the little boy's forehead to make it feel cooler, and he tried to fight down the horror from the death days in the camp that now seemed to be following the canoe. Seemed to be hunting them. A dark beast that he could not see but had come in his dream was now coming with them. At them. To take them.

Go north, Old Carl had told them. Go to where the air was not poisoned, and Leif untied the braided cord from the trees and pushed off and took the paddle in his hands and dug deep into the water. Dug down like he was digging into the earth. Dug down as he was digging for his life. Or dug deep, he thought, as if digging a grave.

Out of the inlet and into the bigger channel the moon-currents were flooding north and he rode them.

Rode them.

Praying for the cleaner air that wasn't poisoned that Old Carl said lay somewhere to the north.

Pushed, ripped, dragged the paddle through the water so that the beautiful cedar canoe had a life of its own, a life without poison air, a life to live, to be.

North.

Without a break. His arms and shoulders and back screaming in agony, but still digging deep and long. Until it came to be later in the day, almost evening, and he found himself weak, weaker, and knew he was getting hot, burning with the death fever.

Leif stopped paddling. He let the moon-currents have them while he leaned to the side and vomited fish and bile and traces of blood into the water—as Little Carl had been doing all day. He could not fight anymore and collapsed and let the fever take him as the moon-currents took them.

Swirling into his mind, his thoughts, his dreams, fevered currents and mind pictures and finally, at last finally, the great and almost joyous release of nothing. Away into no place, no time, no being, no thing.

Away.

And away.

Nothing.

Mother Waters and
Brother Whales

He did not know . . . anything.

For the longest time he only knew, or thought he knew, he was dead. He had gone to that place in the dark world where all was without knowledge or understanding and what he believed was true did not really exist and when that was gone there was nothing to replace what he had been. Replace his life.

He simply did not exist. No dreams, no memories, no anything of what life had been.

He lay in the bottom of the canoe unconscious, unknowing, for a time he could not even fathom. A day into night and then another day into night

and floating, floating back and forth and around, caught in the moon-currents, the canoe a death-bed, where he would die, knew he would die, covered in his own filth, vomiting, finally, just where he lay. Too weak, too soft and weak even to raise up and vomit over the side.

Once his eyes opened briefly and the sun shone down on Little Carl, and Leif could see his gray-ness, see that the little boy's ghost had gone over the bridge but he could do nothing. Could not move. His body racked with bone aches and deep pain, pushing his mind back down into the pit.

And no movement.

A blankness.

And in that, into his unconsciousness, there came the large sound of breathing. It came—though Leif did not know it—from next to the canoe as a pod of the black-and-white whales came near the boat and nudged it, played with it, pushed it back and forth. One and then another of the young ones rose up above the canoe and looked down on Leif and the body of Little Carl in open curiosity but did not find them very interesting, and when one of the mothers made the sound that called to them, they sank back down in the water and moved off.

Young whales, above all, love to play and the young ones did not see danger in the perfect toy—so light and quick to the nose-touch that it slid like a wooden feather on the water—and they were soon back at it, pushing the canoe back and forth across the surface. It was a game they loved, a kind of catch. They played it with a large fish or a small piece of wood, sometimes a small seal, which they'd throw and tail-slap back and forth to one another.

They nudge-pushed the canoe between them across open water, slipping it to and fro on the smooth surface until they came to a small inlet— there were, literally, thousands of such places— surrounded by trees. Here one of the mothers, fed up with their play, came among them, pushed the canoe onto the rocky little beach with a hard shove, and chased the young whales away before any of them could get hung up on the rocky shore-line. Getting stranded on a rock-strewn shore was a great danger for young ones who did not always understand their limitations. It could, and sometimes did, lead to a slow death and this time they caught the urgency in the mother's command and listened and moved out of the inlet.

And the canoe sat.

The canoe as it lay on the shore was a thing of strange beauty. It had been initially made as a dugout craft from a single, straight-grain, no-knotted cedar log. Fire and iron axes had carved out the insides. But after the dugout portion had been completed, the men who made the canoe went back to it from the outside and sculpted it into a lovely, thin-walled, flowing body with a prow formed in the graceful shape of a head showing two carved spirit eyes. The wood on the sides was so carefully carved down that sunlight shone through in a warm red-pink cast, which made it seem almost alive.

If the outside of the canoe was a thing of beauty and graceful joy, its interior was something out of a grotesque nightmare.

Jammed in paralyzed rigor into the bow was the deceased body of the small boy—Little Carl—covered in released stomach and anal gore. While farther back, pushed equally hard into the stern, Leif huddled and, though he was panting shallowly, breathing with great effort in short, soft gasps—he was lying on his face, unconscious, and appeared to be equally dead. As in the bow, the stern's horror-mess around Leif was made up of what had been in his stomach, faint streaks of blood, bile, and bits of smoked fish.

A time passed when Leif could not remember if he had crossed with his ghost over the spirit bridge. Moments when he could not understand what it was to be alive. There would come to be times when he thought of Little Carl, dead, and all the others in the camp, dead, but not him, not fully gone as he knew them to be gone and he felt dipped in shame because he lived while the others died.

In the swirling mass of his fevered madness, living dreams, living nightmares, he thought he might actually be dead, and he did not mind. Could not mind. He believed in the burning guilt of his brain that he was dead and he did not care and he welcomed the end.

Then it began to rain.

This was of course rain country, with thick, dark forests and huge trees, with lush growth so tight you could walk for days without seeing the sky. And streams of fresh, cold water gushed from every opening along the rocky shore, all fed and kept fed by the rains. From fall into winter, rain fell constantly, and unless it turned to snow, the downpour never seemed to stop.

But in late spring and summer, while a heavy rain might sometimes come, generally it did not last long. What fell that day on the canoe was such a rain.

Clean, washing clean, the downpour rinsed everything before it. Leif, struggling to find consciousness, was brought initially to life by the cleaning, cooling rain, and after some small time became more fully awake.

Aware.

Somewhere during the time that the sickness took him—he could not reason nor would he ever be sure how much time had passed—the sickness brought him down and down and down, mentally and physically, until he lay, almost pummeled, on his stomach in the mess that was in the bottom of the canoe.

With great effort he opened his eyes and raised his head slightly and found himself looking directly at the lifeless body of Little Carl. In his delirium he thought he had dreamed it all and was horrified to see it hadn't been a dream, it was real, the little boy was dead.

Some . . . thing, he thought.

Some thing had to be done.

Something.

He tried to rise, to pick himself up in some fashion, but found he was stunningly weak. As if his muscles had become beaten and wounded rags hanging on sticks of bone.

Muster strength. Had to find it, some strength.

Another heave and this time up his arm went and over the side of the canoe. And he hung that way for a gasping breath. Then another. Elbow hooked over the gunwale.

Yet another heave upward and somehow he jerked, a forced, painful twist, and the front half of his body scrambled—almost on its own—to follow the arm over the side and his legs also followed as he rolled like a sack of loose dirt out of the canoe and onto the pebble rocks of the shoreline.

The canoe was only a short way from the water where the mother whale had pushed it—though he did not know of her effort. He wondered vaguely how the canoe had come to be shoved so far up on the shore. He rolled out of the canoe on the side away from the water and lay, catching his breath, then pulled himself in a sliding crawl around the stern and into the water.

He was covered in filth—dried blood and excrement and vomit—and the fresh-cold seawater closed cleanly, wonderfully around him as he lay in the shallows. He wiped his body down with his hands again and again, pushing the dirt away.

Pushing the sick away.

Until all he could feel was clean skin sliding under his palms.

Let the waters, he thought-chanted.

Let the mother waters take it all away.

Away.

Away.

Let the mother waters take it all away.

When at last he felt clean—and chilled, for the

northern waters were always cold—he crawled back to the canoe and using it for a brace, a kind of low crutch, he pulled and forced himself to stand.

Still weak, weaving, he held the top edge of the canoe to steady himself.

He saw again, and would always see in his mind's eye, the body of Little Carl, and moved to try to lift the body out of the canoe. But even as light as it was—Little Carl had taken the full force of the sickness and weighed almost nothing—Leif couldn't do it and stood there, still barely upright over the canoe, hating his weakness. The fact that he lived and was not able . . .

Not able to do.

Anything.

He was ravenous and thirsty and in fact had drunk some mouthfuls of seawater when he was cleaning himself, and while it felt good on his tongue, the saltiness kept it from slaking his thirst. He stagger-walked to one of the small runoff streams, dozens of rainwater rivulets left in the wake of the storm, fell to his knees, and, cupping his hands, drank from the clear, almost sweet, water until his thirst was gone.

Then he rose again to his feet—still difficult, but getting a little easier—and made his way back the short distance to the canoe. There were still several of the chopped-skin strips of smoked fish. They had been safe, away from the mess in the bottom of the canoe, lashed on top of the bundle Old Carl had put in the canoe before making them leave. Leif ripped away some chunks of the smoky red meat and chewed, swallowing them nearly whole. Which he vomited almost immediately. Ate a little more, small bites, well chewed, and kept it down. Then back to the fresh water to drink again, water over the food, feeling the fish and water course through him, fill his body with new-old strength.

To the canoe again.

To Little Carl.

Still weak, but with new strength coming, building, he reached in, took Little Carl up and out in lifting stages, carried him stumbling to the water, and cleaned him as he had cleaned himself, scraping the mess away until the little body was finally clean. Then he wrapped Little Carl in one of the blankets Old Carl had put in the bundle and laid him carefully on the ground.

He sat next to the body, leaning back against the canoe, and did not know what to do next. In the camp they had decided to burn the dead in the small huts, thinking it would help to clean the sick wind left by the men who had lost their shadows. But he could not bring himself to burn the small form wrapped in the soft-coarse blanket. He did not want to leave him here because animals—bears—would find him, and no matter how well hidden he was, they would get to him and . . .

And.

He had to . . .

What?

Had to make it, make it better.

Had to find a place where the bears couldn't get at him.

Had to find a place that the spirit of Little Carl could be found by Odin, a place he could rest and know, know that he would not be disturbed.

His own place.

His . . . what? His . . . where to be safe?

It came to him then. An island. There must be an island away from all, a safe island for Little Carl's spirit to rest peacefully while it left the body and made its way to Valhalla, where surely it would go as all warriors who fought and died went and he had fought the sickness as well and as bravely as any man.

And there were many islands, an uncountable number. It was rumored and said by Old Carl that even this giant land to the west was itself a huge island. That you could not walk across it in a week or more, and that it was so long it could not be measured yet was still an island.

But it was too much. It was a land by itself and had bears and wolves and big cats that moved in the silent, slow curves that wound through the trees and they would find the body of Little Carl.

But if he found a small island . . .

A small island by itself away from shore, too far for bears or wolves to bother swimming to it. An island of his own for Little Carl.

He had more strength now, the strength of purpose, and he removed the bundle and smoked fish, set them aside next to the small wrapped body and slowly dragged the canoe around and into the water, where he tipped it on its side and let the waters come in. Again he used his hands and seawater, pushing the water back and forth and rinsing the filth out until it was almost like new wood.

Then he drained it, tipped it back upright, put Little Carl and the bundle and spare paddle back in, climbed in himself and used his paddle to push it away from shore into the waters of the cove where he turned the canoe about and took deep strokes to get it sliding, get it to move, to dance.

Some thing to do.

A purpose.

Find an island for Little Carl.

Island Currents

It proved not hard to find an island. The main channel between the huge island and the forest to the east that went forever away from the setting sun was full of them.

But to find the right island, the perfect small island, took longer than he expected. And while he felt stronger with his purpose and water and food, he was nowhere near normal yet and it did not take much time for him to weaken. To keep stroking the canoe and trying to fight the swirling moon-currents that flowed and swerved around the islands wore at him until it felt like his arms were going to fall off and his back cave in.

At last he could paddle no more and he leaned back to rest and let the currents take them. And he knew now that the spirit of the boat, and the spirit of Little Carl, and his own spirit had become one. And he thought, the boat has eyes, has our spirits mixed with its own, let it find the way.

Let the Norse spirits find the island.

The sun now was on his back and shoulders and he leaned into the stern and closed his eyes and dozed. Not passed out this time. Not lost in the sickness, but light sleep in the warmth of the sun and the wash of sounds around him. Slow thought, brain-rest, thought-rest—to heal, to open, to be. He had not heard, had not listened to the sounds in days.

Ravens constantly talking, making the throat-words to tell, to tell of Leif and the canoe and the spirits; and crows—forever ravens and crows nearby—with their raucous air-ripping cries that always sounded angry but were sometimes a warning.

Jays rasping. Short words, short jay-words like swearing.

And red squirrels chuckering endlessly, always fussing.

The sounds of forest and sea surrounded the canoe and the spirits as the currents took him along. A kind of music, the way the circling, looping echoes came together, a full music that fed into his spirit. The clicks of crabs and the soft moans of distant whales coming through the sides of the canoe from the sea made a kind of dance. A spirit dance that grew and swelled as long as he kept his eyes closed and let the glory of the blended sounds take him.

But the canoe bumped, stopped gently, and he opened his eyes and found that the sound had lost its rhythm, had gone back to single notes, single cries, and the boat was resting against a small island.

And more, the canoe and moon-current had found a perfect island for Little Carl. Small and compact, nearly in the middle of the main channel, so perfectly round and composed that he could have thrown a stone completely across any part of it. But covered with tall trees alive with jays and crows and ravens in the branches, all complaining about an eagle's nest high up, set in a cradle of forked limbs on one majestic cedar. Most other birds hated eagles—though the mighty white-headed, bald-looking ones ate almost only fish and carrion—and the ravens and crows often attacked them in flight, trying to peck their eyes out. Old Carl had once said it was all in envy, the small birds jealous that they were so small and could not fly as high to soar as the eagles did.

The ghost spirit of Little Carl would never be truly alone, or lonely, on this perfect island, far enough from any nearby landmass that held bears and wolves so they wouldn't spend the time and energy to swim to it.

Leif climbed out onto the rocky shore and

pulled the canoe up above the waterline. Then he reached in and gently lifted the body of Little Carl out and carried it in his arms to the trees where the water would never reach, not even at high tide. At the base of a giant cedar he scooped needles into a gentle, soft bower, and laid Little Carl carefully down, pushed more needles into a warm, soft edge around the little body, like a kind of bed. A cradle.

Back at the canoe he took half of the remaining smoked fish and laid the fish beside Little Carl so his spirit would have food to help him over into Valhalla, and covered him with the blanket.

Then, for the rest of the day, he gathered flat and round stones and built a shelter around and over Little Carl. When the initial shelter was done, he kept going, making trip after trip to the shoreline to gather rocks, and with great care and effort fashioned a cairn of stones over the grave nearly as tall as himself and knew . . .

Knew.

Knew these stones would always be there to mark this place where the ghost of a great young warrior lay, who had bravely fought the battle of the sick air left by the men who lost their shadows and had earned his right to be in Valhalla.

This place.

The Cairn of Little Carl.

For all the time stone could last.

Forever.

Then, spent, he lay back against the stone cairn and let rest take him and slept for a space until the new sun hit his face and awakened him. It was time, he suddenly thought, time to make more of himself.

He moved to the canoe, took out the rest of the bundle, and spread it on the ground. In the chaos and torture and sadness of The Sick, as he had come to think of it, and the deep sorrow of the loss of Little Carl, he had not paid attention to anything practical. He had been ready for death, had set himself to be prepared for death.

But not for living.

And now it was time.

Old Carl had not had long to prepare the canoe for a long voyage. Or for any voyage at all. The Sick, the poisoned air, was all around and the crew had been dropping as if cut down by a weapon. There was the sudden horror of a man leaning over as he helped another dying man, catching the sickness, and dropping in his own death on top of the dead man. Everybody was ending so fast there had been no time to gather everything needed for what now faced Leif.

He looked down at what he had.

A hand ax, Old Carl's own that he'd had on the ship. The knife at his belt, a worn blade with a wooden handle that Old Carl had given him when another man was going to throw it over the side. Leif sometimes had missed his father—or perhaps an imaginary thought-picture of him since he had never seen him—as he missed and had never seen his mother. And Old Carl had told him, "You have no father to give you a knife so this one you may have from me." In addition to the copper pot, there were four fishhooks stuck in the side of a coiled-up roll of corded, braided line, the four-pronged head for a fish-spear or seal-harpoon, two woolen blankets—smelling a thick, almost chewable odor that was a mix of sheep from the original wool, never washed, and the stink of many men, and fish and salt air— and a small leather pouch. In the pouch was a short piece of hammered steel, about as long and thick as a large man's finger, and an oblong-shaped chunk of black flint with sharp edges—steel and flint to make sparks for starting fires. There was also a pullover anorak, so tightly woven that the lanolin oil in the coarse unwashed wool made it nearly waterproof.

That and the clothes he was wearing—rough, tattered cotton sea trousers and a sailcloth pullover shirt. The fabric, now stiff and uncomfortable from repeated saltwater soakings, was useless at holding body heat. It was summer now, early summer, but fall would come, then winter, and these thin clothes would not keep him warm.

These clothes, these few tools and supplies— that was all he had.

No, wait. Most important. He was not quite alone.

He had the canoe. And the canoe spirit.

They would be with him. They had found the perfect island for Little Carl. They would help him.

He stood and moved to the canoe but something in him did not want to leave the Little Carl island and he stopped, wondering at his own thoughts, why they kept him.

There was more to do, in some way. Something more.

To sing.

It jumped into his mind as if the thought were pushed.

He should sing a song to honor Little Carl . . .

He turned back to the material of the bundle

and took the small pouch with the flint and striker iron. In the woods, away from the sea and behind the cairn, he had seen an old fallen and rotted tree. Too thick and wet to burn, he knew, but under it he would find what he needed.

Along and beneath the dead tree, he dug with his fingers in the soft dirt, and in moments came upon an old ground-squirrel nest. It had not been used recently—he smelled it and made sure there was no odor of fresh squirrel urine—and he scooped out the nest and formed it into a ball in his hand. The squirrel had made the nest out of small, fragile bits of dry grass, woven together with plucked hair until it was a fluffy, round sphere with a small cavity in the middle.

It was as if the squirrel had purposely made a dry clump of tinder to use for starting a fire. While it was slightly damp around the edges it had been mostly sheltered beneath the dead tree and the center was bone-dry and he knew it would accept fire.

Leif tucked it into his shirt and gathered thin, dry dead limbs broken from the lower parts of the trees until he had firewood enough for a small fire. He then cleared a small circle by the cairn and arranged the twigs in a kind of pyramid—tent-shaped—with a narrow slot in the side to reach into the middle. Then he squatted back on his doubled legs and took the strike-steel and flint from the pouch.

He had done this many times, had learned to make fire almost before he walked—for starting the cooking fires in the brick stoves on the boats—and he put the squirrel nest on the ground, held the steel directly over it, and deftly struck it with the edge of the flint. One strike, nothing; second strike, just one spark; and when the steel was ready a third strike, and a small shower of sparks fell into the nest. Most fell to the side and went out cold but a few went into the hole in the center and began to glow as they hit the dry grass and hair.

He picked up the nest quickly, cupping it to shelter it from the breeze that came off the water, and blew softly, ever so gently down into the sparks, blowing, blowing, until the glow brightened more and more, and then burst into a small flame.

Swiftly he pushed the burning nest into the middle of the pyramid of twigs and continued to blow, slightly harder now but steady until the flames grew and grew, and took the wood and brought it into flame as well.

Then more wood, and more, until he had a comfortable fire going. He pushed back on his haunches, to get his breath, and then stood to gather more wood. When all was settled he leaned against the cairn and felt the spirit of the fire surround him, warm him, clean him in some way the water had not cleaned him and he tried to think of a song for Little Carl.

At first it did not come. Would not come.

But he remembered, let himself remember

before The Sick, remembered Little Carl, on small fat legs, trying to dance around a cook fire, mimicking some of the Norse chant-dancing the men had done. He fell and fell again and again but he kept getting up to dance.

Getting up.

Getting up to fight the part of the dance that kept making him fall.

Getting up again and again as if the falling meant nothing, could mean nothing as important as getting up.

Getting up to fight.

Getting up to fight The Sick.

Until.

Until in the end, and it was the end, he could not get up again but he fought, fought all the way down until his ghost had gone from the body and his spirit had gone over to the dreaming place just before Valhalla and the body could not fight more but the spirit could, would fight forever because of where it had started.

In him.

In Little Carl the fighting spirit was born and would always be.

The fighting-spirit song of Little Carl.

The Getting Up song.

Yet when Leif put more wood on the fire and began to compose the song in his mind so it would grow into the thought-pictures that it took to make a good song of honor, he found he could not sing it.

He tried. Started with high notes, eagle notes, and words to make pictures:

SEE HIM DANCING
AROUND THE FIRE ON SMALL LEGS.
    SEE HIM DANCING
    AROUND THE FIRE ON WARRIOR'S LEGS.
        SEE HIM DANCING
        AROUND THE FIRE WITH A WARRIOR'S
        HEART.
            SEE HIM DANCING

AROUND THE FIRE TO RISE.
　　TO RISE UP
　　TO RISE UP
　　TO ALWAYS RISE UP
SEE HIM DANCING
SEE HIM DANCING
SEE HIM DANCING.
TO ALWAYS RISE UP
　　AND FIGHT.
　　　　TO VALHALLA.

But only the high note, the beginning note of the honor song, came and he could not sing more. His throat closed and when he tried to open it, to make the chant-song come, it brought out thought-pictures of how it had all been in the good time. All his thought-pictures were . . .

Of memories. How the camp had been before The Sick. How it had been when the men were happy and had good food and full cheeks and smiles and songs and dances and the camp seemed to come alive in his mind, a camp from before, before . . .

Before it all ended. All died. When he pushed at it and tried and tried to sing, to chant, all that came was what jammed in his thickened throat and he could not sing. He sat, staring into the fire, and felt only sadness that brought again the dark shame that he had lived and all others had died.

And with the sadness and shame came yearning thoughts of going back to see, to see if there was still part of that time left. Knowing he could not, would not, because Old Carl was a man who knew things, knew all things, was always wise and right and had said to never come back.

Never find that time again but keep going.

North.

With all that in his mind he leaned back against the cairn, felt the closeness of the round rocks in and on his back and finally allowed the heavy exhaustion to take him into a deep and complete, dreamless sleep.

Whale Song

Jays awakened him.

Blunt, raucous, sharp blasts of crude sound cut into his sleep and took him up and into the sun. They were angry about something, as jays always seemed angry, and he thought for a moment—and worried—that it sounded like their bear warnings and swearing complaints. Then he remembered the small island he was on and that no bears would bother to swim to it and he stood, stiffly, made his way to the tiny stream, and drank until he was filled with the cold, nearly sweet clean water. He was instantly ripped with hunger, which was in itself not particularly new.

He seemed always to be hungry. But there were only a few bites of the smoked fish left and after he ate it the taste of the fish seemed to make his hunger worse.

He had to find food. He made certain the fire was completely burned out, took one last look around the island of Little Carl, and moved to the canoe. It took but a moment to load the small number of possessions in the little bundle, which he tucked up into the bow, pulled the canoe around—lifting it so it wouldn't be gouged on the rocks—floated it in the shallows, then hopped in and went to his knees while he picked up the paddle.

One, two thrusts biting deep into the water and the canoe came to life and glided away from shore. He let it coast for a space and found himself looking back at the cairn until the canoe caught the current, moved out of the inlet and was carried around a point that blocked vison so the cairn was gone from sight.

He turned back to the front and paddled, adding to the northern flow of the moon-current. He kept pulling hard, fighting images of the cairn, fighting sadness, until his lower arms started to ache. Then he let the current have him again and admitted the hunger. That feeling had gone for a bit but came back now with a vengeance and he was acutely aware that he had eaten all the smoked fish and that his stomach was moving viciously toward his backbone.

He would have to find food soon.

He was traveling north on the side of the main channel between the big island and the forest that went forever and there were constant openings to inlets and coves. Some were fairly shallow, only going back into the forest for a few hundred paces. But some were much deeper, winding far out of sight. The problem with many of them was that the trees came down to the water's edge in an abrupt manner, sitting atop a sheer rock wall.

What he was looking for now was a place where

a heavy stream or small river came out into the sea and left a gravel bar covered with brush and willows, and the only way to find such a place was to go into each of the deep clefts until he could see the end.

He picked the first deep opening and started in. He was lucky and found that it went in a long way—the current was flooding at this time and carried him along as well as paddling—ending in just such a sweeping gravel pan.

But before he moved that far—perhaps halfway in—on the north side of the inlet the land sloped down gradually to a rocky ledge. Just after the first wide bend there was a large stand of blackberry bushes so thick some of the plants actually hung over the side of the shore into the water, making a rich green tunnel.

The berries were ripe, hanging heavily on each thorny branch within easy reach. He nosed the canoe under the overhang so that some of the branches were hanging into the canoe, and ignoring the stings from the thorns he took handfuls of berries and—caught up in his hunger—didn't even chew but swallowed them whole.

They were so sweet they made his jaws ache.

He kept eating them until his gut rumbled and turned over to tell him to slow down. He did so, but kept eating the berries, squeezing them now against the roof of his mouth with his tongue so the juice came out of each berry like a sweet drink.

He did not know that he had been a long time at the berries until he felt the current running into the inlet change, starting to head out, and he had to hold on to the bushes to keep from being pulled out of the inlet.

Still he kept eating, holding the canoe in place with one hand while gathering berries with the other until at last the edge of his hunger seemed to lose some of its sharpness. He was not full. He thought then he would never be truly full again. But there was some control and as his frantic pace at grabbing and eating slowed, he came suddenly to find he was not alone.

He should have known sooner. Should have been aware. There were signs, indications, wiggling bushes, a thick, dark smell. But filled with hunger and need, he had not seen or felt or smelled the signs.

Now he heard a scuffling sound on the ledge behind him and turned his head to find he was staring full on, directly, into the face of a black bear.

The bear did not seem surprised but just looked at him. Studied him. And its stillness and look started the boy's brain working through what he knew, or thought he knew, or had heard what people knew, or thought they knew, and talked around fires of their knowledge.

Stories.

That bears were like people. Thought like people. Had good times and bad times as people had good and bad times. Were sometimes happy and sometimes angry and that nothing was worse than an angry bear except perhaps when the earth shook and sent giant waves against the world. The boy had never seen such waves but Old Carl talked of them and had great respect for them and said you could not fight them.

Just as you could not fight bears.

And Old Carl said that all bears were not the same. There were black bears and some of them became red when they grew old and their hair changed color, and there were brown bears that were twice as big as black bears and were often angry when there was no apparent reason. One would rip a whole log apart to find a single grub worm to eat.

An entire log.

And he said that no bears liked to be stared at and the very worst thing was if a mother bear even thought you might endanger her cubs with so much as a glance, nothing could save you. Leif now moved his eyes from the bear and looked down into the canoe, then off to the side away from the bear and for a long time did not move, was as absolutely non-staring-still as he could be. Not even breathing.

Then came a soft snort and a rustle of leaves and he looked back to see the bear moving off into the thicket, eating berries as it slowly shuffled away.

So, he thought. Not a mother. No cubs. And not angry or feeling that Leif was eating berries that belonged to the bear—a thought that had crept into his mind during the three or four lifetimes he waited for what might happen if the bear decided to jump down on him in the canoe.

Soon even the sound of the bear moving was gone and the smell—the dark odor that at last the boy smelled and should have smelled sooner— was diminished and he relaxed, almost idly picked more berries and ate them. He knew he needed more than berries and wondered why his stomach had seemed to desert him and wanted to get shed of the berries when he first saw the bear. He had as a matter of living seen bears before—although never one close as this, so close he could have reached out and touched it—yet his stomach flopped over inside his gut when he saw the bear's face and it was all he could do to keep it from emptying. You'd think, he thought, his belly would be glad to have some berries and not be so eager to get rid of them.

Still, Leif held them down and let the canoe move away from the overhanging berries and into the current. It was still running the wrong way—heading out toward the main channel—for what he wanted, but the strength of the moving water was slackening and he knew it would soon stop moving before it started back in. So he paddled against it for a time, moving farther into the inlet but slowly, and then, when the current was reduced to slack water, picking up speed until he rounded a small point and saw the end.

It was exactly what he was trying to find—a

small, shallow river-creek pushing through a gravel bar into the open water. On either side there were more blackberry bushes—they seemed, indeed, to be everywhere the soil was anything but pure rock—and more important, stands of straight willows, most of them small enough to be almost tall wands, but some stood as big as his wrist and taller than he stood, which was what he was seeking.

And no bears.

He beached the canoe on the gravel and hopped out. There were odd piles of bear scat here and there, but all were old and dried out. He took the hand ax and moved into the willows. What he was after was a tall willow that was straight and about a finger's length in diameter. When he found one he cut it off near the ground and carried it back to the canoe. There he cut it to about twice as tall as he was and used his knife to peel the bark. It was slick and gave way easily and stripping the bark only took him a short while, sitting on a large rock near the edge of the stream.

Once peeled, he laid it on some rocks that kept it off the ground and in the direct sunlight and while the moist film left by the bark was drying he paused to drink out of the stream. Again, he had not really been listening—though the run-in with the bear should have made him more alert—and now he once more heard the gurgling sound of ravens talking and jays swearing over the rippling of the stream.

He was sure it all meant something, especially the sound of the ravens talking to one another and wondered if it was possible to learn their language enough to understand what they said.

Still, the sounds—even the complaining of the jays, and now and then the *chukker* of a red squirrel—did not seem to signal anything of alarm, or urgency, and he let himself sit and lean back against the side of the canoe and enjoy letting the sun cover him.

Slight doze. Not deep, nor hard, but enough to feel rested and hungry—the break gave his stomach time to finish off the berries he had eaten—and he found the willow had dried enough to allow him to work on it.

Using the knife he sharpened the slightly thick end into a kind of truncated point. Then he split the end exactly in the middle so it could be opened slightly.

Into this split he inserted the metal tang from the end of the spear head Old Carl had put in the canoe and then wrapped it snugly with thick cord from the ball of woven net twine that came in the bundle. This he pulled and tied off as tightly as he could pull using his teeth and when it was done he could not move the steel point no matter how he pulled on it.

So he had a fish spear.

Though the fish were not running like they would later in the season, in shoals so thick you could nearly walk on them, there were always some strays caught in the shallow pools. Leif waded in to stand knee-deep in the cold stream as still as he could with just the tip of the spear down in the water.

He waited. The roiling current made shadows that whirled here and there like fish and twice he almost tried to spear one of them but held back, held back until what fish that were truly there became accustomed to his legs and body being in the water.

Then a silver flash rolled in next to his ankles and he lunged with the spear.

And missed. Thrust higher than the body of the fish and he realized that the water altered the placement of the salmon. It wasn't where it appeared to be but slightly lower. He had to thrust not at the top of the back of the fish but toward the bottom edge for the spear to catch the middle of the body.

More waiting.

Finally—his legs were turning bluish from the cold—another whip of silver appeared, this time slightly farther away, almost directly beneath the submerged spear point and he lunged again, aiming the downward thrust at the lower edge of the salmon, felt the soft-thick thud of the spear point going into flesh and twisted it so the barb would hold. Then he pulled the fish sideways to shore, not lifting it yet for fear the weight would make it fall from the spear, and flopped the fish up on the gravel.

It was a fine silver-sided female salmon. A little longer than his arm—heavy and fat—and he killed it with a round rock to the head and when the fish was still he cut it open with his belt knife. She had some eggs, perfectly round and pinkish red, and he stripped them out onto a flat rock. He knew they would make a good soup—had eaten it many times—but he was so hungry that he ate some raw, and when they had settled on top of what was left of the blackberries, he turned back to the fish.

He thought of building a fire and using the copper pot to make a fish stew but that would take time and there was a slight breeze working back into the woods. There would be smell now, the blood smell of the dead fish, fresh because he had opened it, and that would travel fast on the breeze. And if he took time to cook, to boil water into a fish stew, the hot cooking smell from the steam would also catch the wind and move into the forest.

Pulling.

Pulling.

And the bear from the blackberry stand was probably not too far away. Certainly close enough to catch a thick blood smell on the wind and it would come and take his meal . . .

No. He put the fish in the canoe, turned it and pushed off into the inlet. He would find a small island and cook the fish there, and if not, he could eat it raw, cutting the rich red meat off in strips, dipping them once in the sea to get a slightly salty taste, and eating them—as Old Carl had often said—plain and clean.

Soon enough he found a place on the main shoreline that he considered more or less isolated—he thought perhaps far enough from the bear in the berry patch to be safe—and pulled up on the edge. It took him just moments to find another dry, unused mouse nest beneath a rotten log, spark a fire in the nest, add wood, and sit down to a meal by the fire.

He cleaned the salmon—setting the liver aside for soup later—and put the whole fish on a flat rock propped up and leaned toward the fire so the heat from the flames cooked the meat. When one side was done—the skin peeling away—he flipped the fish over and cooked the other side, and when that was done he lowered the rock flat, used it like a small table, lifted the skin from the meat, and pulled the tender pink flesh away from the bones.

He had never tasted anything so wonderful. It was like pouring something new inside his body—which had in the sickness, he felt, become something impossibly old—and he kept swallowing the meat whole, not taking time to chew, letting the fish slide into his stomach. The meat was oily with fat and he could feel the grease move into his arms and legs and chest like rich, soft fire.

When it was done, when he had eaten all the meat, he ate the eyes—which had their own salty taste—and then put the leftovers, liver, skin, and skeleton into the copper pot, added seawater, and with more wood brought it to a boil. When it made a soup with the head and skin and fins, he took it aside, let it cool, and drank the whole thing without putting it down.

Then sleep.

He pulled the canoe completely onto the shoreline, sat down next to it, leaned against the side, and dozed.

Small dreams.

One of Little Carl running around the camp looking for something. He could not tell what it was but everybody was laughing and smiling and they seemed to have something the little boy wanted.

Short dream of a bear stealing his berries, just

reaching again and again with hairy arms and long-clawed paws, eating all the blackberries in the world before Leif could get to them.

And a small dream of his mother. He had dreamed the mother dream many times and it was always the same. She was with some other people, talking to them—he heard her voice as muffled sounds that were almost words—and she always had her back to him so Leif could not . . . quite . . . see her face. Just there, just the edge, but never quite enough to see. Short, quick dream.

Then another of orcas playing with his canoe and him lying in it while they pushed it back and forth. It seemed very real and he thought it may be but could not openly remember it happening. Still, he thought of them as a form of whale brothers—with breath that smelled of rotten fish—and in the dream did not mind them playing with him.

As a toy.

Then no dreams and just sleep, stomach wrapped around blackberries and greasy fish meat and salty soup, warm and filling.

A blanket inside his stomach.

Wind Music

Sunshine.

Cutting in on him, hot, making his lips crack, and awakening him to see a raven poking his head inside the cooking pot, picking at the fishbones and skeleton of the fish head.

The big bird gurgle-squawked when Leif shifted and jumped back but did not fly off. He had grabbed at the fish head when he moved away and walked back and forth near the waterline in a strut, carrying the fish head up in front as he marched.

It's like he was showing off, Leif thought. Proud of getting the head for himself. He even put it down and pretended to pick at it, though there was nothing left but the bone-shell of the skull with teeth and eye sockets, and then took it up again and flew with it to a nearby branch.

More gurgle-talk from the limb, again parading back and forth up there, and finally he flew off and scornfully dropped the head in the water. Leif stood. He wanted to stay here and take time to refresh even more—take another fish or two and smoke them—but he had cooked and the smell of flavorful steam would have gone up and out in the trees and willows.

He thought the black bear would certainly come. He had gone a fair distance from the bear in the berries, but he felt the smoke and smell would carry forever. It was actually a little strange that the bear had not shown by this time. So Leif put his gear in the canoe and slid off into the water. The current was flowing slightly out of the inlet, so he took a few strokes and let the current take him. He had not gone a stone's throw when he looked back and saw the bear.

Or more accurately, two bears. Both black bears, not large, and they were investigating the campsite. One of them, the smaller, took a few tentative steps into the water toward the canoe, pushed by curiosity, but it was for show. Leif was too far out by this time, the water so deep the bear would have to swim, and it was clearly not worth the effort. The bear snorted—a *whuff*—and returned to where Leif had made his cooking fire. Leif had poured water to make certain it was extinguished, but the sludge from the ashes had the smell of cooking and the flat rock he had initially used for baking was covered with fish grease and blood-juice stains. The bears tussled with each other to decide who got the chance to lick the rock and muck about in the ashes, but aided by a couple of blunt swipes with a large paw, the bigger bear won by default before it became a full-on fight.

The bear scene vanished as the canoe rounded

a point and Leif returned to paddling. He was getting better, stronger. Not there yet, not back to normal, but with the sun hitting his back and the water flat and calm, he took deep strokes with the paddle and felt the strength come into his shoulders and back and arms. Heat from the sun, rest from his dream sleep, and muscle from the salmon grease and berries flowed into him as he swung out of the inlet and headed north, the canoe moving because it was connected to his arms, his arms to his shoulders, his shoulders to his back, and all of it to his mind, his thinking . . .

Not there yet.

But coming, coming.

For just that moment, looking ahead up the main channel with thick woods on the east and more forest far off across the channel to the west on the big island, for just that moment in the sun and the good weight of digging the paddle deep in the water, feeling the canoe slip forward with each stroke . . .

For just that moment he only thought ahead. Only saw and felt and smelled the beauty, the joy of what was coming and not the gray, not the darkness and horror of what he had left behind.

For just that moment he thought ahead, wondered ahead, smiled in his thoughts ahead.

Then the gray seemed to close in, come back again, cloud his thinking once more like a sullen mind-storm, and he had to stop it, stop the gray thinking, and the only way he knew to stop it was to think of what came next.

He didn't think he could just move from this spot to the next spot without thinking, without knowing . . .

He had to have some kind of thought for action.

Move north, Old Carl had said, move north where the death sickness couldn't follow them. Only now it was just him.

But north was a direction, not a place.

You could, he thought, go north forever and not get to a place.

And there it was—maybe that's what Old Carl meant.

Don't go to a place. Go to be. Just to be.

And he chanted with the sweep-pull of the paddle:

GO NORTH FOREVER.
LIKE THE WIND.
THE NORTHWIND.
GO TO BE THE WIND.
THE NORTHWIND.
THE NORTHWIND.

The smooth chant helped, settled him in some way, made him less frustrated and he was just becoming accustomed to it, to himself.

When he was suddenly not alone.

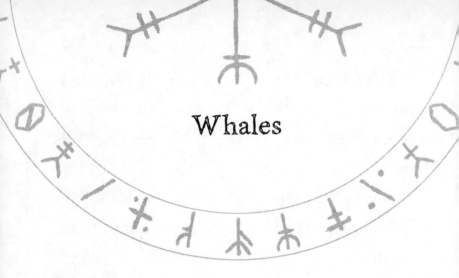

Whales

Orcas.

Beautiful black-and-white markings, dorsal fins breaking the surface all around the canoe, they seemed to come out of nowhere and surround him. He could not exactly tell the number of them because they rolled under, back and forth, and beneath one another, but it was at least six, maybe eight of them. Some large—one he thought male, though he wasn't sure, seemed huge, much longer than the canoe, with a large dorsal fin sticking straight up—some smaller, and possibly two or three young ones.

I should, he thought . . . I should be afraid

of these killer whales. They could easily slap or ram the canoe and break it to pieces. He had seen them slap-throw small seals back and forth through the air at each other until the seal was clearly floppy in death. Several times he had watched them offshore near the camp playing so roughly with one another he could feel-hear the sudden blows from the beach.

And he somehow dream-remembered them playing with the canoe, shoving it this way and that, when he was sick. Obviously they had considered him and his canoe little more than a toy and if they had started to play rough with him . . .

He should be afraid. At least concerned.

Yet he was not. Something was distinctly not threatening about them, and even when two young ones came over and started to nose the canoe back and forth they did not seem to be very serious about it. Mildly curious. Playful. Were these the same ones that were with him when he was sick?

He was struck by how they looked. Almost stunningly beautiful. They shone black and white in the clear cold water with lines so clean and sharp they looked carved or drawn. Swimming without any obvious effort, sliding through the water next to the canoe, and he wasn't sure whether he was keeping up with them or they were holding back to match his speed and remain with him. Even the big one seemed to stay near him, coming up to blow not a paddle's length from the side of the canoe, blowing so that his warm spray that smelled sharply of fish came over Leif in a fine mist.

They were a family and the whole family stayed with him, or seemed to. Or perhaps he stayed with them.

However it was, he did not mind. He in fact thought of them as friends—knowing at the same time how that seemed a little ridiculous— yet came to understand and believe that they wouldn't hurt him.

And yet.

Yet they worked around him and he remained among them, however it happened, until they curved into an inlet. There was such purpose in how they moved that it was evident to Leif that they had meant to come to this one place all along and he almost automatically—nudged by the young ones—followed them in.

How could he not? he thought. It was right there. How could he not?

At the far end of the inlet there was a shallow, sloping shore that came down into the water a good distance and it was covered with small round stones, none bigger than his fist. Thousands, millions of them formed a thick layer from the shore down to the sea bottom, a huge carpet of stones carved and pushed by endless wave movement and tidal flow until they were so polished they shone when he picked one up.

It turned out to be these stones the whales were after and Leif paddled the canoe off to the side and watched them as they took turns diving and sliding across the stone bed on their stomachs and sides amid great clicks and chukker sounds he could hear-sense-feel through the sides and bottom of the canoe.

At first he thought they were just playing and indeed they seemed to enjoy the feel of the small pebbles. They would roll and slide over one another, teasing, and take turns moving to the eastern side of the U-shaped shoreline and slide-roll across on their bellies or sides, arching their backs as they moved almost as if being petted.

But there was more to it than just a game. They seemed to have such a definite purpose that when he watched more closely he could see they were using the rocks in some way. Perhaps to clean their sides and belly. They were carefully moving their bodies, rolling from side to side, rubbing at the inlet's bottom with their faces, back down to their tails, flukes, and even these they carefully dragged across the stones.

And when the adults were done, they worked at teaching the young ones, who had been watching but not trying, to go to the end of the inlet and start passing and rolling across. Initially they simply didn't understand and would go the wrong way, or head out of the inlet, or forget to roll, or just do one side, or pick up one of the stones and head-flip it skittering across the surface and try to hit it with their tail. They were, Leif thought, like a pack of young dogs and he laughed out loud until he noticed that one of the whales, the big male—perhaps hearing the sound of his laugh—moved slowly away from the juveniles and stopped, lying right next to the canoe, almost touching, so that his body was between the canoe and the rest of the pod who were still trying to get the youngsters—Leif actually thought of them as pups—to start using the rocks correctly.

And there he stayed.

Not being aggressive, nor even threatening.

Just there.

Protecting.

As he lay, the spume of his exhaled breath came across the canoe, across Leif, and he smelled it again as he had before, the rich thickness of it, smelling of fish and salt air and something deeper, warmth, personal heat from inside the big animal, a way Leif could know more about the whale. The signature of his breath, the private inside of him, and as he lay, still, breathing slowly but in sharp gasps, his large dorsal fin was next to the center of the canoe. Right next to Leif. The fin standing shiny and glistening black next to the canoe, just an arm's length away. Right there.

Right . . . there.

I should touch it, Leif thought. I should touch his fin and perhaps he could know me, know more about me, as I would know more about him. But he held back, not afraid but more embarrassed, as if it would be an intrusion, a meddling. What right did he have to interrupt what the whale was doing, thinking, by sticking a hand out and touching him, a giant animal gentle and kind enough to leave the boy alone in his canoe? What right did he have to reach out with his puny arm and silly hand to touch that dorsal fin pointing at the sky with shining pride? What right?

But still, he thought. Still . . .

How can I not?

There it was—the hot worm of thinking. It reminded him of the time he first learned to make fire with flint and steel into an old squirrel nest. The single spark, growing like a red worm, feeding on bits of dried grass, growing, growing until the first tiny tendrils of flame caught the tinder.

Almost the same thing. The hot worm of his thoughts, a nudge of a glow, feeding on thought and more thought, a glow of wanting, a small flame of needing, to know, to know more, be more . . .

This close, at this most perfect moment, how could he not touch the whale?

And his hand, almost by itself, moved out of the canoe, across a short space—but across much more than that, he thought, across two different worlds—and his fingers and thumb lightly, gently, grasped the trailing edge of that rigid fin.

For a moment.

Just that. A moment.

Then he let go and pulled his hand back. Thought on how it felt. Hard, harder than he thought it would be—like a live, shiny black stone—and slick. Maybe a little warm, though he couldn't be sure because it was wet.

Not sure what to expect. Would the whale be mad? Upset? Would the whale destroy his canoe? Flip just one powerful time those huge flukes and slap him out of the water?

What he did, or didn't, do completely surprised the boy. The whale slightly raised his head, rolled a bit so he could see Leif sitting there—looked directly at the boy with his eye,

eye to eyes—and rolled back and remained as he was, lying there.

Protecting.

Then the whale exhaled suddenly and the boy breathed in at the same time. Leif had been holding his breath the whole time without thinking and took air deep now, inhaling some of the exhaled breath of the whale that came over him, breathing in the warm, inside smell of the whale and the odor mixed with the touch on the fin and he wished they could speak to each other, wished he could ask the whale . . .

What? Ask the whale what?

Ask him about everything. All things a whale would, could know that he himself wanted to know and understand and he said aloud softly: "I wish . . ."

Then he stopped. Not knowing what he would wish, what he wanted to know. And instead of the wishing came a sense of wonder. There had been this . . . this thing, this moment when the whale knew him and saw him and understood that Leif meant no harm and he, the boy, had seen that the whale meant him no harm as well and they were just there.

The two of them. Right there alongside each other, knowing that about themselves, that they meant no harm to each other.

It was a kind of talk. There was that. Some kind of talking.

Not words, nor songs, but an open knowing had passed between them, and Leif knew that he would never lose that, never forget that knowing, for the rest of his life and hoped it would be the same for the whale. With that knowledge he came to believe they were friends. No. More and less than that. On one side of the fin there was a small diagonal, dimpled scar, no longer than the boy's hand, and he knew that if he saw that scar again he would know the whale, would know he had passed knowledge to that individual whale and this same whale had passed some of his thinking, his being, to Leif . . .

Not a friendship, exactly. But next to it. Close to it. And he thought he would stay in the inlet with the whales for the time being because he enjoyed their company, liked this whale's company.

But in a few moments they were done with the pebble beach and with the young ones' rolling and playing and they all turned and, again with purpose in their movement, made their way out of the inlet and disappeared around the point into the channel.

Gone.

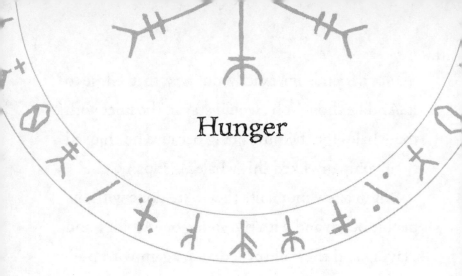

Hunger

He took purpose from the whales.

They were gone, moving at a much higher speed than he could ever master with the canoe and he knew, or thought he knew, that he would probably never see them again.

But he took the same purpose.

He was to go north. To become the same as the northwind. To always travel north and he stroked out of the inlet and turned east to start in that direction. But late in the day a wind had come up, out of the northwest so that he was paddling into the wind, and the moon-currents took him slightly back until it seemed that no matter how hard and fast he paddled he was almost going backward.

It became clear that with nature against him he could not move forward very well, and he went into the next inlet to the east that presented itself to wait out the wind and current.

This inlet was more a deep canyon, with steep sides, that went in a long way and ended in a slightly curved, narrow stone-ledged outlet. A stream cut across the side of it and spilled into the sea. It did not have a gravelly fan to its front but as he drew closer he could see salmon pushing up into the rapids that flowed over a rocky edge. They were not in a full run, thick together with backs nearly touching, but certainly enough to allow him to take some and fill his cavernous-feeling gut. Here and there in the brush that led up and away from the steep-sided stream there were blackberry bushes. Although not as numerous as the ones he had worked before, the deep color of the berries hanging in the brush—added to the sight of the salmon nosing at the stream outlet—made him almost weak with hunger.

No bears. He could see no bears nor sign, even old sign.

Still, bears were potentially everywhere, both black and the giant brown bears. And because of the inlet's layout, if he tied off to the brush and went in any distance, he could be caught dead-cold away from escape.

It was of course possible a bear would not hurt him—as had happened with the black bear he had come face-to-face with in the berry patch earlier—but it was not something he wanted to chance and if it did happen to turn sour . . .

He needed a way to get in and get out quickly. Grab and run, he thought, and in the same moment he realized he didn't have to leave the canoe. He could come in on top of the salmon trying to swim up into the creek, work over the side with the spear until he had several in the boat, then paddle out of the inlet to find a more deserted, small—bear-free—island to make a fire and eat and smoke fish and sleep.

Which is exactly, or nearly exactly, how it worked, or could have worked . . .

He nosed the canoe against the rocky bank, pushing forward just hard enough to raise the bow a little and keep it in place on the rocks. Beneath him the salmon rolled and pushed to get into the mouth of the stream, and he leaned carefully over the side, held the spear's point down in the water, and when a salmon presented itself, hesitating and holding for just an instant, Leif slashed down with the spear and took the fish just in back of the head.

It seemed to stiffen with shock and before it could start wriggling, he swung the fish up and over and inside the canoe. With a twist of the wooden shaft, he plucked the barbed point out of the fish, left it flopping, went back to peering over the side and quickly took another one.

At this time, and suddenly, their numbers grew rapidly, explosively, as if the fish were in a frantic panic. They were running so jammed together he could almost hit without aiming—like a carpet of live fish, some even slamming into the bottom of the canoe—and he took four more, silver sides flashing in the sun, before he heard the distinctive *whoosh* of an exhaling whale and turned to see he was all at once most decidedly not alone.

Killer whales. Again.

As before he was not sure of the number. Four or six, perhaps, and he couldn't initially identify them. Just the same clean lines as they took air and he could see their beauty through the clear water. But finally, one rolled and when the dorsal fin moved past the rear of the canoe he saw the diagonal scar and knew it was the same one he had touched previously.

They had talked, had known each other, and Leif felt a brief pleasure after expecting never to see them again.

Only this time it was different. Vastly different. There was not the playful air about their coming. None of the rolling on the bottom rocks or trying to keep the young ones in line.

They were there to hunt, to kill, to eat, and they went about it with a calculating, practiced—cold-blooded, savagely focused—force that came suddenly, as suddenly as the fish going into panic, and it was clear that nothing outside the hunt, the killing, the eating mattered. He had no time, half a moment, to make a startled sound and then it was as if Leif, the canoe, were not even there—were in fact only another obstacle to overcome and they promptly did just that and simply nosed and shouldered the canoe out of the way. They did it so abruptly, and roughly, that he nearly capsized, slid jaggedly across the water away from the rocky ledge and out where it was deeper, and still farther out until he was well away from what they were doing.

Then the whales moved in, between where he

tossed wildly in the canoe and the rocky ledge, and set to work. The rocky shore and the steep walls on either side made a large U-shape, and two whales, the big male and another slightly smaller one, went back and forth across the opening of this U, blowing bubbles that made a kind of bubble-wall or net.

Leif realized they were herding the salmon with this bubble net, pushing them up into the curve of the U, packing them in, getting the area tighter and tighter, smaller, until the water seemed to be boiling with fish.

When the salmon were jammed in on top of one another the whales took turns sweeping through them, grabbing them in their jaws, feeding until they were full, whereupon the ones who had been eating moved out to take over and keep the bubble net working while the original net workers went in to feed.

It was beautiful teamwork, the boy thought. A kind of dance, with whales rolling into the fish in sweeping curves, hitting through the massed salmon, rolling out and the next coming in. A dance, and he was thinking of making it into a chant-song, and would have, except he was suddenly distracted by still more company.

Eagles.

And ravens.

And smaller birds, jays, and some he had not seen before . . .

It was the eating habits of the whales that brought them. He wasn't sure why, but Leif thought that with an animal as large as a killer whale, eating a fish as relatively small as a salmon, the whale would just swallow the salmon whole and let digestion sort it out.

But no. After stunning a group of the jammed salmon with a heavy tail-slap they would eat the ones that lay still by coming at them sideways and easily—deftly—biting the middle out of each fish, swallowing the juicy meat and some of the entrails in the center, letting the tail and head float away separately. Some of these leftover bits sank but a good portion of the mess floated to the surface . . .

And that brought the eagles, who must have been watching, waiting, and seemed to come from all directions. They were just beautiful—especially the mature ones with dark brown bodies and majestic white heads—and had wing-spans that seemed as wide as Leif's outspread arms. Leif tried to count them, but as with the whales there were too many moving and mixing, and an accurate number became impossible. Ten, twenty eagles, he thought, diving down from the trees, and neatly, artfully dropping their talons as they soared only slightly above water to scoop up fish heads and entrails to carry away to gobble down on a tree limb or the rocky shore.

But they never seemed to be satisfied and rather than just eat what they had grabbed they would look to what other eagles had taken and go for their gutty treasure instead of their own.

Soon there were open fights, wide-winged and screeching battles with talons ripping at each other, fish guts and fish heads flying through the air, dropping down and draping across the tops of those same majestic white heads.

Adding to this wild chaos came the truly clever ones—the ravens. They worked among the eagles, some going in close to get an eagle's attention, hopping and short-flying at their heads to distract them while other ravens, apparently preselected, waiting patiently, dodged in and took the fish heads or tails or guts from the eagles, many pausing mid-theft to poke at the eagles' eyes.

It became a swirling mass—above and below water—of whales, salmon, eagles, ravens, hopping and flying jays, and some waterbirds the boy had never seen before, diving into the center of it all to bring offal up from the water that other birds would grab, and all was slashing, flying fish guts and heads and tails and screeching eagles and squawking ravens and whale tail-flukes slamming explosively down on the salmon in the water . . .

In all of this, the canoe had been freely drifting. Without thinking, Leif moved to safety, stroking the paddle, carefully balancing the canoe with his knees to keep from capsizing as the whales rolled nearby and the eagles dove so close to him that he had to duck to keep from being hit by a wing.

One eagle actually perched on the bow of the canoe to eat fish guts. But the instant a raven stole the morsel away from him, the eagle turned and, spying the dead salmon in the bottom of the canoe where Leif had put them, jumped down. Sinking its talons into one of the fish, the eagle tried to fly away, but the fish was too heavy to allow it a quick escape and Leif clipped the bird with the flat of the paddle. It dropped the salmon, screeched at Leif, and flew back into the fray.

In a few moments, Leif had worked out to a place slightly farther away from the action.

Clear. And he sat there at the side, balancing

the still-plunging and rolling canoe and tried to see it all, understand it all, follow all that was happening, but there was too much and it overloaded his vision, his thinking.

Finally he just sat, nearly as stunned as the salmon, reeling with the violence of what he saw.

Then, as suddenly as it had started, it ended. The whales veered off, swam out of the inlet; the eagles and ravens flew off, holding in talons what food they could carry; even the smaller birds vanished back up into the trees.

Except for some stains on the rocks, it was as if it had never happened, as if there had never been what Leif decided was a battle. A battle for food and he realized suddenly that aside from the whales and possibly the ravens—both of which seemed to have other things happening for them, like humor, thoughtfulness, slyness, affection—hunger, pure raw hunger was the driving force of everything in nature. Anger, of course, but anger based on hunger, and in the same thought, looking down at the dead salmon he had speared and would eat, he decided he did not want only that in his life. For his life.

Did not want to be only hungry.

Go north, be north, but see and be more than just what I shove in my stomach.

See past the hunger.

See past.

See . . .

The Cook Camp

Another island—away from the mass of land to the east and across the channel to the dark loom of the big island on the west that was so huge it didn't really seem like an island— hopefully, probably, safe from the bears.

This island, though small enough to stand alone, was large enough to have several small inlets of its own, and Leif picked one on the north side and nosed into it. It was only two or three stone's throws deep but at its end there was a small pebble beach and a trickle of a stream filtering through the rocks. Above the rocks there was a sand-gravel pan, and he pulled the canoe up, well out of the water, upside down on this sand-and-gravel mix.

He had noticed the canoe seemed to be getting heavier, the cedar was soaking up water, and he wanted to give it a chance to dry out a bit during the two or three days he would be here smoking fish.

First a camp.

It was starting to get foggy and he took time to gather firewood before it became difficult to see well. This took a while and then it started to sprinkle and he spent still more time finding a dry mouse nest to use for tinder under a large piece of bark.

Everything felt damp and he had trouble getting the spark to flame in the nest and he had to make new sparks four times to get a small bit of fire. When at last it did flare up he had more trouble getting the flame to feed and grow on twigs so that he could make a decent fire with larger pieces.

Finally, with the fire going well—he could hear the mist sizzle as the sprinkling rain dropped on the flames—he cut long green willows from along the bank to make an angle-shaped drying rack. These he formed in a rough triangle, jamming one end of each willow in the ground, leaning inward and coming together in a point up and over the firepit, well above where the flames could reach, and he put in five crosspieces jammed in forks to make the rack.

Not as good as the large racks the men had made in the fish camp, but it would serve for this smaller load.

The dead fish he had placed on the gravel and he now used his knife to split them open. One had eggs, which he promptly ate raw with a little salt water for garnish—hunger taking him—and one whole salmon, the one the eagle had grabbed and torn a bit, with the guts and head removed, he set on a slanted flat rock and leaned in to the fire to cook.

The rest he split, leaving the sides connected at the head, and turned them inside out, slashed cuts across the red meat to allow them to dry more readily, and hung them, meat side out, on the drying rack he had made over the fire. On the fire he threw some green grass and leaves to make smoke, which the heat powered up through the drying fish and kept the flies—now moving in as they smelled guts and meat—from landing on the fish and planting eggs that would quickly become maggots. In the copper pot he placed seawater—for the salty taste—and the livers and some remaining eggs and the head off the one fish he was cooking on the slanted rock. The pot he placed directly in the flames to make a stew.

It took only a short time for the fish on the rock to cook—or at least cook enough—and he eagerly ate it with his fingers, tearing the meat off the skeletal structure, and these bones and the crisp skin, he also put in the stew pot, scales and all.

Belly full of meat, he added more wood to keep

the fire going, put more green weeds and leaves on to make smoke, drank handfuls of water from the stream until his stomach bulged with it and then went looking for berries.

There were not the huge stands he had seen in other places but alongside the trickling stream he found smaller clumps of berry bushes. Perhaps because they were not as many and took more time to pick, the blackberries seemed to taste especially sweet and rich, as if each berry was a special treat. He picked until his lips and fingers were stained dark and the berries had mixed with the water and salmon in his belly when he paused and nearly fell asleep on his feet.

He was totally exhausted—numb and bone-weary—and would have to lie down and doze soon or he thought he might pass out.

It was still drizzling, or at least heavily misting, and he went back to the fire, added still more firewood and green material to generate smoke, then set about making a shelter.

The canoe he had turned upside down and he now propped one end on a large boulder so it formed a kind of narrow lean-to. Along the sides of the tipped-up canoe he placed pieces of wood, jammed into the gravel and pushing up against the upside-down edge. All this to keep the canoe from rolling over if a wind came up. When it was secure, he put his blanket and gear beneath the canoe, spread the blanket—which was damp but not soaked—and positioned it so part of it was tucked in under the stern, which was resting directly on the gravel, and made a serviceable bed.

Another look to the fire, adding still more wood and green leaves and grass, and he crawled under the canoe, lay on half the blanket, pulled the other half over himself, and was asleep in little more than moments.

A dream. He dreamed of Little Carl who was not dead but somehow alive, dancing a step-dance schottische around the fire while the men laughed and clapped in rhythm to his steps.

His legs were too short to make the dance work right—especially the hopping part—but nobody cared and the little boy was laughing and suddenly Leif's mother was there. In the dream she was tall and straight and had long hair but he could not see her face, wanted her to turn so he could see what she looked like, wanted to move around in the dream to see her, know more about her. But it was not to work. Little Carl kept dancing while the men clapped the step-tune and the dream became not so happy. Grated on his thinking.

And he jerked awake, opened his eyes in irritation because he had not been able to see his mother's face and immediately discovered once more that he was not alone.

Ravens were there, around the fire and the drying rack. The flames were nearly gone and only a trickle of smoke went up through the meat, and the ravens sat around the fireplace and drying rack like a bunch of old men. Feathers fluffed to avoid the mist, waiting for the smoke to be completely gone so they could hit the meat on the drying strips.

"Aaargh!" Leif grunt-growled and pitched a rock at the ravens. None were hit and they only slightly startled at the bouncing stone and his sudden growl, and didn't fly off but simply dodged out of the way.

Two of them—there were eight and others, Leif couldn't tell how many, in the trees around the campsite—separated from the group and came sidling toward him and it became apparent they were there to lead Leif away from the rest.

A plan, he thought. As with the whales. The two ravens had a plan and were going to "work" Leif and keep him away from the drying fish while the others fed.

Well, he thought, no.

"No!"

He said it aloud and rolled out from under the canoe, stood and made his way to the firepit. The wood he had stacked nearby had been hit with the mist and the top sticks were damp but he found some beneath that were fairly dry and he soon had the fire going again. He put more leaves and grass to make smoke and drank some of the fish soup from the pot.

It was amazing to him that the ravens didn't fly off. In the fish camp with the men they would fly away when the men swore and threw rocks or sticks at them, but here they just moved off and stood on rocks or gravel, burbling to one another.

Waiting.

And again, Leif wondered what they were saying. The sounds were changing all the time, sometimes almost a whisper, then again an open squawk or a long string of gurgling throat noises. They meant something, some words, to one another.

Wait, he will sleep again and we can get the food.

He is a silly creature who will forget to watch us.

Wait.

Perhaps, Leif thought. Something like that.

Or possibly scorn. Sometimes their tone of voice seemed on the edge of insulting. Scornful little statements.

Look at the poor weakling—he can't even fly.

See how ugly. Just bare skin. He has no feathers to catch the sun and shine and keep out the weather.

I will have to stay awake more, he thought, take better care of the fire and smoke or I won't have anything to eat. There will be nothing but fat ravens.

At least the rain-mist had stopped and he sat close enough to the fire to dry out his hair and blanket and damp cotton clothing.

He had a sudden intense memory of life on the many ships on which he had been shuffled one to the next as crew. Or more accurately, a kind of galley thrall. Always down below, working at menial tasks: sewing; cooking oily meat for the crews; emptying buckets of filth when the weather was too rough for the men to relieve themselves over the side and had to use the wooden buckets;

dodging beatings that any man on the crew could administer to him for any reason whatsoever. One of the worst thumpings—it left him bent double for a week—was when he forgot to store the sewing needles in the cooking oil and they had started to rust. And always, always damp. Never dry clothes. Damp with salt in the creases so he had a continual rash in his armpits and crotch.

And here he could feel the cloth drying as he never felt it on the ships.

And no beatings now.

Danger, perhaps, or certainly. Bears and the ocean could kill. But no beatings.

And it was all up to him. He could eat or starve, depending on his own actions, his own thoughts, his own plans.

The same as the whales.

Or the ravens.

Or any living thing. From whales down to mice. All thinking. All taking care of themselves, by themselves, for themselves . . .

He stood to check the meat on the racks and was surprised to see that the cut slabs had dried considerably in the short time he'd hung them over the smoke and fire.

Seeing the pink meat brought his hunger roaring up once again and he tore away a sizable chunk and bit off strips that he swallowed nearly whole. He was still hungry and thought of eating more but decided to save it for what he now considered it to be: canoe meat. Traveling meat. Something to eat while he paddled north.

Instead, while the meat was smoke-drying he took the spear and made his way to where the small creek, fed by seeping springs on the island, trickled into the sea. He found the water there as clear as sight and—as he stood in the shallows— colder than he had felt previously. Made his toes curl under. There were no salmon schooling in large numbers or trying to run up the creek, but there were always salmon nearby, moving in the shallows, and he learned to wait.

Wait.

With the tip of the spear down in the water, unmoving, and his legs and upper body as still as a rock, a tree, in moments the fish had come to believe he had always been there, was part of the bottom, and moved in close to him.

Closer.

Then, aiming at the bottom edge of a good-size silver he powered down with just wrist-and-arm movement, took the fish cleanly through the middle, twisted the spear to get its barbs in solid, and dragged the fish up onshore.

Quick, sudden strike with a rock to kill it, then back to the fire where he used his knife to open the fish, split to expose the meat, cooking on a flat stone facing into the fire, put the liver—it was a male so there were no eggs—and head into the pot for stew, added some seawater, which he sloshed into the pot at the shoreline, shoved the pot into the fire.

Added more wood. More grass and leaves to

make smoke to keep the flies—and the ravens, who were still there, waiting, some on the ground and others in the trees—away from the drying meat . . .

Then leaned back against a large rock by the fire and listened to the ravens gurgle-talk.

The sun came out from the clouds. The mist-rain was gone. Warm on his face and his belly all tucked in with good meat and some blackberries he had found and it was just . . . exactly . . . right.

A perfect moment.

He should make it last. In some way, there must be a way, to make it last, or lodge in his mind so when things weren't quite perfect he could remember this moment, could call it up.

And he thought it would make a good chant-song, a chant-song to go with paddling the canoe. Or even a dance, a shield dance, but then decided they were both too temporary. There had to be a better way, some thing more lasting, permanent. If he had a chisel he could chip his story in stone or if he knew more he could make a rune stone. But he had no chisel nor a way to make one. He would have to think of a different way . . .

And he knew. It came to him like the growing spark in the tinder. Same way. He needed to draw it. No, he had no way to paint or draw the story.

But he had a knife.

And wood.

More wood than could even be measured. There were old cedar logs everywhere and he could use the hand ax to hack off a flattened piece and smooth it by scrubbing it with sand and carve the story.

No. Carve the moments. Carve the pictures from his mind that would make a story. His story.

Carve his memories in wood.

Current Sliding

There came a time when he did not think of the future.

The sun warmed him, he moved the canoe north, not hurrying but often letting the tidal motion take him along and when it went the wrong way—south—he simply tied up to shore and napped or carved on a plank he had chopped out of a cedar log until the current reversed. When the dried meat supply grew low, he would move into an inlet, take some salmon, eat his fill, dry the rest, head out, and move north again.

Because it didn't become completely dark at night—just a grayer day—he did not think in terms of time. All he knew was the canoe and the forest sliding by, and keeping his belly full of salmon and blackberries.

And that he was getting stronger. With the growing strength came the returning knowledge that he had been—literally—deathly sick. Had seen Little Carl die and thought he was also dying. To come back . . .

Back from that to being able to paddle the cedar canoe, take fish, eat berries, move north, was something he at first thought would be impossible yet now found himself doing with more and more purpose and force.

Still not all the way back to normal. But getting there, closer and closer, and feeling the core of him getting stronger sometimes dazed him. He would sit in the drifting canoe, riding the current, just watching the forest slide by slowly, and carve on his story board, as he came to think of it, in private wonder.

Except that he couldn't really call it private

since he was never truly alone. Ravens were with him constantly, flying near him, sitting in trees as he passed, flying ahead to watch him as he drifted by them. On more than one occasion a raven would land on the front of the canoe as the eagle had done, and eye his stock of dried salmon carefully. As if adding it up in some way, calculating how much salmon he had and then fly off gurgle-talking to other ravens.

Talking about me. And my food. Making fun of me.

Nor were the ravens the only ones near him. While the eagles didn't come as close to him as the ravens they would swoop down just over him, then out in front of the canoe, dip to the surface of the water, and snatch a fish. Leif was surprised at how often they would clutch a fish that was too heavy and have to drop it back in the water, and even when they made a successful grip on a salmon they could handle they would have to align it carefully, head forward, tail back, to streamline it because they couldn't fly with the weight hanging sideways.

Add to all this the intermittent flock of crows that would appear flying next to and around the eagles carrying the fish, trying to peck out the eyes of the large birds of prey. Often an eagle—especially the younger ones who did not yet have their white heads—would become frustrated and angry at the smaller black birds and drop their fish and have to go back, still accompanied by the flock of vengeful crows, and try to get another fish.

Into this mess came jays and smaller birds, looking for potential scraps, so that there was a constant swirling cloud of birds, large and small, rotating around and above the canoe. The birds seemed to take delight in releasing their scat on the canoe. And on Leif. And he was constantly scooping up seawater to slosh in his hair to get the mess washed out.

At intervals—and there seemed to be no

rhyme nor reason for it—all the birds except the ravens would leave. He decided that it was as if the flocks of crows and small birds and even eagles had specific territories, and Leif would move through each of them in the canoe and there would be relative quiet until he moved into the next territory.

He also noted that the ravens did not seem to be bound by territories, or if they were, couldn't care less what other birds might consider proper. He recognized some of them, who had discolored wing or back feathers marking them, and saw that they stayed with him no matter how far he moved. Indeed, when he stopped to sleep for a time, tied to a branch onshore, he would doze over the dried salmon to protect it and when he awakened the same birds would be there.

He saw killer whales almost constantly. They were always making their way north out in the main channel so he wasn't close enough to see if he recognized or knew any of them.

But he saw them most every day, moving past him, and he wondered—something he seemed to be doing all the time, wondering—why they all seemed to be heading north. It could not be for the same reason as Leif was moving, running from The Sick, from sick death, but as he moved, day on day, anytime he saw them they were working their way north. With apparent intent and purpose. And as with Leif, while they didn't seem to be hurrying—he watched several times when they stopped and bubble-netted (as Leif thought of it) salmon in the ends of inlets and fed—yet they were always moving north. Backs rolling, dorsal fins sliding, spouts of misty exhale in the air, sliding north.

Nor were there other whales. He had seen other whales in the distance off the ships he was kept on and marveled at the giant size of their flukes when they dove but there were none here, moving even in the main channel.

Only the black-and-white killer whales and

Sliding Currents

It was the same current that he had come to ride, to know, the current he thought he understood that brought him to the edge of disaster.

Or actually a mix of currents.

He had found there were many thousands of islands, small and large. And he had come to use some of them as temporary, bear-free stopping places to dry the canoe and smoke salmon and boil soup-stew.

He had not thought much of the placement of the islands. They were just there. And if he had considered it at all, where they were and what they meant, he would have skipped over it as being unimportant to his welfare.

Nature put them there, or Odin, or the sea, and that was it. Where they were didn't matter.

Except . . .

And the *except* could be lethal.

The islands and inlets were everywhere. Too numerous to count, really. But though they seemed separate from one another, scattered, so it seemed, all over the place, they were all part of an enormous living kind of ocean being, all interacting with one another.

And the tide.

And the island-and-inlet placement became critical. As the tide, the moon-current, pulled the water around the islands and up into the inlets, the flow—the massive flow—of the current was structured and limited, sometimes slowed, other times pushed hard around curves, until it came upon high tide and all the places were as filled with sea as they could be.

But not all at the same time. The filling was different depending on location, on length of inlet, on size of islands so that it took a relatively long time for all the tidal-filling to occur.

And when it finally had happened, there was a brief time when everything was static. Flood tide.

Then the tide fell and the water started to run back out of the inlets.

And the placement of some islands and inlets became vitally important. In most areas there would just be a simple current flowing outward and it was only a matter of tethering the canoe to shore or paddling across or with the current.

But sometimes the current coming out of one inlet would move more rapidly than the current sweeping by out in a channel, causing the waters to curve, and curve again, moving stronger and stronger in a circle that would soon begin a small circling tidal flow. But then, feeding on itself, eating more and more passing current, it would change its character. It would grow into a monster. An enormous ripping, sinking, savage whirlpool.

If the tide had been very high, and larger-than-usual amounts of seawater were involved, these whirlpools could be huge, clawing all nearby things in the water into the middle and without mercy sucking everything into a killing, downward spiral.

Leif did not know any of this.

Not yet.

He was asleep, sound asleep in the bottom of the canoe with his head on the blanket roll. He had used a piece of cord to tie the blanket in a tight bundle enclosing his meager equipment because he had found that when he dozed, slept, the ravens grew bolder and would try to get inside the blanket. The smoked fish he kept next to him as he slept, with his arm over the meat, and sometimes the ravens were so forward they would peck at the meat next to his arm.

But the sun was warm, the bottom of the canoe cozy, a rocking cradle of motion, and Leif was out completely—

And would have died that way were it not for a raven sitting on the edge of the canoe over the meat. This raven was more bold than the rest, or perhaps more hungry, and it decided to grab a large piece of meat off the slabs of salmon, but the meat was heavy and stuck to the skin and when the bird jerked at the fish, it was off-balance and fell, flapping wildly, directly on Leif's face.

Leif snapped awake and the raven flew off and the boy started to lie back down but hesitated when he realized the movement of the canoe felt oddly changed. It was moving faster than normal—he could see the trees in a distant shoreline dashing past—and he sat up to see what had changed.

At first, for a moment, he could not understand what he was seeing. The canoe was caught on the outer edge of what appeared to be an enormous circular current, a spinning pool of water, which, to Leif, made no sense at all.

How could it be there?

Strange, but he did not perceive a critical danger.

Yet.

He rolled to his knees and grabbed his paddle. He was still far from the circle's center and it seemed to be a mere matter of paddling away from the pulling motion of water.

He dug in, swinging the nose of the canoe, aiming away from the center, moving, he thought, across the direction of the current that swept the canoe along.

Plenty of time.

He thought.

But no. The canoe was directed outward, but no matter how hard he paddled, the canoe seemed locked in the current.

Aimed well out, yet no matter how strongly Leif paddled, the canoe kept moving sideways around the huge circle, drawing closer toward the center.

Trapped? he thought. *But how can this be happening?*

He tried even harder, ripping at the water, fighting the pull but nothing he did worked. He tore the paddle through the water, tore until his arms, shoulders, back were on fire but none of it helped.

Out of the corner of his eye he saw a huge dead tree in the center of the circle suddenly rise vertically, slash back and forth—it seemed to be waving at Leif with its scraggly black branches, calling to him to come with it down into the dark places—and then vanish in a gulp as the current sucked it down.

He used up everything that was in him, his core strength, his very life forces, and it did no good. The canoe, caught in the ever-stronger, tighter circular current, was grabbed like nothing more than a floating stick, a leaf, and now, no matter what he did, he could not change what was coming.

The ripping of the whirling pool set up other smaller but equally strong crosscurrents, and one of them clutched the canoe and flipped it over before Leif could think, could even believe he was in the water.

He grabbed at the side of the canoe. It was filled with water but still floating. As a log would float. The blanket roll was floating nearby and he tried to get a hand on it but failed as it swirled away.

And now . . .

Now he could do nothing. He was in the water, clinging to the side of a mostly submerged piece of wood that had been his canoe, and was instantly convinced that he had no chance. That his life force must end now.

All end . . .

All to end.

Around him everything began to happen more rapidly. Trees off to the side looked to be a blur as the current swept Leif and the canoe closer toward the center. Faster and faster until he was near the core of the beast—he felt he could even hear it now. Growling waters. Waters with teeth to pull, to cut, to kill.

Now he could feel it. Pulling on his legs like claws. Swirling him into the center to pull him down, down into an end, as it tore his hands from the canoe and dragged him down in a spray of bubbles that was his air leaving. His life leaving. Forever.

And he surrendered—knew he was done, would end here, would see Little Carl and the mystery of Valhalla. He surrendered as he was pulled deeper and deeper until all he could be was some errant thoughts, flashes of memory, and then a blank grayness and he would die . . .

Die.

And it stopped. As rapidly as it had started, the currents lost their circling force as the tide ended and the whirlpool disappeared.

Just in that way. That quickly.

It stopped and he rose unknowing, unfeeling, rose like a piece of wood, not thinking, until his head broke the surface and he hacked water out of his throat, his lungs, and sucked in such gasps of air it sounded like a killer whale spouting.

"Aaarrrgggh!"

And he was not dead, not ended, could hear the sound he made and could see the trees and feel the air.

Sweet air.

Air made of honey.

And close by was the canoe, also disgorged by the current, and farther away but floating enough so he could see it was the blanket bundle. The canoe was right side up, though full of water, and he found the tie rope from the bow and pulled it—struggling with the effort—toward the blanket bundle. Here he jammed the wet bundle into the submerged canoe and put the tie cord in his teeth and started working toward shore. He found this did not work very well—the canoe barely moved—so he spit out the cord, went around to the stern, and started to push.

It was still terribly slow, hard work. The small

craft hardly moved. But pushing it was at least slightly better than pulling it with his teeth and he aimed it generally toward the shore—which seemed an impossible distance away—and tried to build a rhythm to his kicking and pushing.

Lunge, kick, lunge-kick . . .

A time passed, a seeming lifetime of cold water and aching muscles, and in this time he found himself lost in thought. Where had the monster come from; how did it work? Why didn't he die—yet again? Could it be his fates, Odin, taking a hand and wanting him to live? And here he smiled. Broken, tired, teetering on the edge of being sick of it all, sick of traveling north, sick of pushing this stubborn, sunken canoe through the water, he smiled. And thought, *perhaps I'm part eel and easy to puke up. That might be what saved me. Eel blood in my veins and the water found me easy to puke back up* . . .

Nonsense thoughts. Lunge, kick, think, lunge-kick-think.

And finally—and he thought it was truly final;

he seemed to have nothing left—he felt, almost sensed, the bow of the canoe bump against a shore and he looked up and ahead to see an island.

He found as he lowered his legs his feet came to rest on the bottom and the water was only waist-deep. Rocky, gravelly bottom that felt wonderful, and he stood and worked the canoe onto the shore—a gravel-and-rock beach—rolled it to dump the water, untied the spare paddle he thankfully had tied into the bow and put it on the rocks to dry. Spread the blanket to dry as well and took a moment to evaluate what he had lost.

His spear was gone. He had somehow not tied it in with cord. And of course all the smoked fish—and his story board—that had been sucked out by the water.

But that was it. Not bad.

He would have to get food soon—hunger was already pulling at him—and he would, but now he had to rest. Any conceivable reserve he might have had was gone, used up pushing the canoe to shore, and he lay on his stomach on the gravel warmed by the sun, put his cheek on his hands, and closed his eyes. One blink open, then shut again.

And he slept.

Changes; Skin to Wood
to Water to Become

Hunger tore at him now.

He had slept—had deeply core-rested—for a long time. Time enough to dream of a dark tunnel that was pulling him down to what Old Carl had called the caves of screams where vicious god-beasts ripped flesh from the bleached bones of cowards.

He'd awakened just as he was taken up and out of the pit of dreams by a giant hand—again, the hand of Odin?—and was instantly so hungry, he put two pebbles in his mouth to give his tongue something to do, then had to keep his throat from swallowing them to get something in his cavernous stomach.

The spear was gone but he found a stand of willows and made a new shaft. He had no steel point—the only one he had vanished with the fish spear in the whirlpool—but he had seen Old Carl fashion a spear from wood.

He cut the shaft longer than Old Carl was tall, peeled the bark and let it dry in the sun. When it was no longer sap-slick, he used his knife to split the large end partway down, jammed a piece of wood into the split to make a fork with the two tines about a hand's width apart.

With the size where he wanted it to be he used cord to lash the cross-stick in place, which made the tines rigid. Then he carefully sharpened each of the points with his knife until they would draw blood if he pushed his finger against them.

And he had a fish spear again.

He made his way out into the gravel beds where he could see fish moving and stood, waiting, until they had accepted him as a new part of the water.

At last one came in range and he jammed the

spear down, felt it hit solid meat and thought he had a fish. Had food.

But the wooden points were not barbed and when he tried to lift the salmon from the stream it slipped off the spear and escaped.

He shook his head. Had to be a new way. The points were scuffed a bit from hitting gravel beneath the fish and he sharpened them with his knife and went back to the water.

More waiting. The violent wriggling of the salmon he speared had made other fish move away and it took time for them to come back, and in those still moments he realized that there was silence.

It wasn't that there had been wild noise before but there had been the constant cawing of crows, gurgling of ravens, and chatter of other birds.

But now it was silent.

Suddenly dead, cold silent.

All he heard was the rippling of water around his legs, and he turned and let his eyes move in a circle around the line of trees and water.

Nothing was there.

But still, silence.

The hairs on the back of his neck rose and a spiral . . . spiral-something went down his spine and came back up.

Then he saw it.

No, saw-felt it. Leaves moved on willows in a way that put them unnaturally against the direction of the breeze that moved up from shore.

And in there, back in the leaves and low limbs on trees, he saw a motion, also against the breeze. And at the center of the motion there was a deep, dark spot and small cloud of thick brown—a place of no-light—and without sound or warning an enormous brown bear stepped away from the trees and stood looking at Leif.

And Leif thought, *Oh.*

Just that.

Then, *No.*

It's not a bear. It can't be a bear. It's too big to be natural. If it stood . . . if it stood, it would block the sun.

He had never actually seen a brown bear, had only heard stories about them from men on the ships, but always assumed the stories were all sailor's lie-stories. Stories told to make men look . . . bigger. Smarter. Braver.

But this wasn't a story.

It was a mountain of a bear, easily two or three times the size of the largest black bears he had seen.

And it was looking directly at Leif. No. Into Leif, through Leif, as if Leif wasn't there. Or didn't matter.

Leif flicked his eyes to the canoe upside down on the beach. Impossibly far to get to, to escape into the water. Without moving his head—something in his thinking strongly suggested it was best to not move—he let his gaze swing up into the trees. No help there—he would never reach them. Then back out to the water. He could move in that direction—try to dive in and swim away but if the bear only half tried it would have caught Leif before the water was past his waist.

The bear was too close.

Too close.

If the bear wanted him, there was simply nothing Leif could do to stop him. And a strange thing happened: He relaxed.

There was really nothing to worry about—it was like the weather. Worrying did no good at all. The bear was like a possible storm and if it took Leif it would be the same as if a squall wind had come and blown the boy away.

The Sick had not killed him. He had not starved to death. The whirlpool had puked him up like eel meat. He had been in violent storms on the ships that held him work-captive. If Odin wanted him, there had been many opportunities to take him.

The same now.

It wasn't up to the bear, really. It was up to fate, Odin, Leif's luck.

So he relaxed. The hair went down on his neck. His breathing returned to normal and he relaxed. Then, still without moving, he waited.

And studied the bear. It moved toward the drying blanket, the canoe, whuffling the ground with its nose as it moved and Leif was astonished at how little sound it made. It must have weighed as much as many men together and yet there wasn't even the tiniest sound when its paws hit the ground.

And it was incredibly fat with amazingly thick and luxurious fur that seemed to ripple when it walked, pushed by the fat just under the skin. When the fur caught the sun it shone with a near-gold color—as the seal furs shone—and when the bear grew closer Leif could see insects flying about the long hairs of the fur.

It stopped at the blanket and with one long claw—with careful, impossible dexterity—it lifted the blanket, smelled beneath it, and flicked it to the side.

Then the smaller pieces—the ball of cord, the hand ax, the pouch with his steel and flint, it examined carefully, turning them over with tiny motions from the enormous claw—it smelled, then snorted and moved to the canoe.

Here the bear smelled the inside, idly licked at a stain, used one paw to flip the canoe over, and smelled the bottom and when that was done, turned, and stood at the edge of the water and looked at Leif, who was standing knee-deep about five paces from the bear.

And Leif thought: *If I die here, it is my fault. I should know about bears.*

He let his eyes whip past the bear, saw scattered bits of not-quite-dry bear dung here and there. Small piles he had not noticed.

But I was tired. Pushing the canoe endlessly after the whirlpool. Too tired to even see the bear sign? I should have gotten back in the canoe and gone to a safe place to rest. To fish. To live.

To live.

It was all there. All I had to do was look. Open my eyes and look. See.

And now the bear stood. Leif's fate, his future, stood a few steps away, studying him.

Measuring me.

And it is all my fault.

It was all there and I didn't see it because . . .

Because I'm a damn fool.

And he thought finally, on top of all the other thoughts: *Because I don't fit in. I am here, but not here. I am not real to this place.*

I have been only passing through.

Now the bear snorted—Leif could smell its breath: rotten fish, maybe a tooth gone bad, some berries—and moved its head sideways back and forth with the nose raised, the mouth a little open.

To smell me better. To air-taste me.

But suddenly with a grunt the bear turned and walked away, vanished still without a sound in the surrounding trees and was gone. As if it had never existed.

A ghost bear.

But no. It had been real.

He knew it by the feel of his knees that, on their own, weakened and lowered him into the water.

It had been a real bear.

And it could have killed me. Eaten me. Did not maybe because it was too full of salmon—had been working at a run and eaten its fill—or just luck. It could have ended what I am or ever could be.

Because I, Leif, did not fit in.

Was not part of where I am, part of the trees and sea and wind and whales and, yes, the bear as well.

He should have been part of it all but he was just passing through.

And he made a vow now to Odin:

I will join with and of this place.

I will see.

And learn.

And know this place and all places that will come to me.

With this silent vow, and a deeper understanding, he wrapped the blanket—now dry—in a bundle with the pot and ax and cord, his meager all—and tied them into the canoe. Then he slid the craft into the water, jumped in with the paddle, and worked away, staying near the shore—as he would always try to do—in case there was another unexpected whirlpool.

He paddled a good part of the day and he didn't sleep in the canoe and he studied each place that became available to stop and take fish, studied the ground and listened to the birds for the sudden silence that meant something . . . always meant something.

When he at last came to a place where a small stream came out across a gravel-rock bed and there was no bear sign, he stopped, pulled the canoe up on the gravel, but close to the water so if he needed to make a quick escape it was available.

Then he took fish with the wooden spear—marveling that he had not dropped the spear when he first saw the brown bear—pinning the fish to the bottom and sliding them up on the shore rather than trying to lift them out.

When he had five good silver-sided salmon, he put them in the canoe, moved back into the stream and opened one of the females and ate a handful of eggs. Just to cut the hunger.

With his catch he traveled along the shore until he came to an island isolated enough to avoid bear, where he stopped, made a fire, a drying rack, put a pot of fish stew-soup cooking and sat near the fire to keep away the ravens and crows, which had come with him when they saw the dead fish and started moving closer to the racks.

He cooked one whole salmon and ate the entire fish when it was just slightly steaming, warm enough to enhance the taste, licking the salty fish oil from his fingers before he leaned back and let his mind roll on.

Had to do a new story board. Different, too. He had started the first one by just carving single items—a killer whale, a salmon—no story there. Just pictures. Needed more. Needed to show how it all started. The fish camp. The death ship. Old Carl. Had to find some berries, too. Berries on top of the salmon made a good gut feast. Berries . . . and he saw the bear pause and eat green grass. Seemed odd. But if a bear ate grass maybe Leif should try it. Add some grass to the fish soup. Berries, stories, fish, grass, stew . . .

And he slept again.

Safe this time.

He awakened at intervals to add wood and grass to the smoke fire to keep the ravens from the meat. They were openly brazen now. Walking around like chickens.

Leif wondered how they would taste but put that thought away. He had fish. Ravens were probably tough and stringy. That's if he some-how caught one. They were cagey enough to get away from him, and besides, he was getting used to them, liked having them around, listening to them talking to one another . . .

Rested, finally, then back on the water. Found berries and ate them until the berries added to the salmon made his stomach feel like a drum. Packed tight.

Carefully, along the shore, in and out across shallow inlets, quickly paddling across deeper ones that sometimes went in farther than he could see, he worked north.

Now there is no line that separates me from the canoe, from what I have become. The boat is my skin and body and mind and I am the water and wood and the sun and the birds.

All one.

All together as one. I am part of it now.

Part of all of it.

I have become.

Heartbeat; Sea Pulse

Almost a routine now.

He paddled until he grew tired. Then he would find another safe island, and either set up a camp or tie the canoe to shore tree branches and sleep in the boat.

When he became hungry he would eat. If he were low on food, he would stop and find a stream with no bear droppings—feeling he had used up all his luck with bears—and take fish. If the spear broke—which happened frequently—he would simply make another. If he were hungry for more than fish, he would eat berries and if there were no berries, he would make a fish stew and put in bits of chopped grass—the same kind the bear had eaten—and turn it into a vegetable-fish soup.

Sometimes he would stop for a day or two and make a proper camp with a resting fire and a bed of cedar limbs beneath the canoe, and pull the canoe up to let it dry. In this he had to be cautious to not dry the canoe too much. In several places very tiny cracks would appear if the wood became too dry and he didn't want them to grow large enough to become problems.

To everything, he found, there was a balance. Dry, but not too dry. Take fish to smoke when he was hungry but not too many, lest they spoil. A balance. Paddle until he became tired, then rest.

He worked on the story board when he was taking a long stop to dry the canoe. He started with a carving of the fish camp and the death ship coming and was working on a smaller story-picture of Little Carl dancing—hard because of the memories—when he suddenly wondered why he was doing the stories at all.

But he kept working on them, even with the wondering, and finally decided it didn't matter what happened to them later, or why he was doing them. They were done because what had happened to him, the movement of his life, was there in the wood. The stories on the board were life itself. When he was done with them, or part of them, they were like permanent memories and whether anybody else saw them, or understood them . . . didn't matter.

They were carved memories.

Just that. The stories were themselves and that's all that mattered.

And so he kept working on the carvings when he made long stops. Then, too, he had normal work that was necessary. He had lost one paddle during the whirlpool and when he found a dried split of cedar on a dead tree, he fashioned a flattened board that he axed and carved into a spare paddle. When it was carved to shape he polished it by rubbing the wood with handfuls of wet sand—as he polished the memory carvings— until it was smooth, then tied it securely into the bottom of the canoe along with the blanket bundle and other equipment. He saw, had seen many other whirlpools—although none as big as the one that had captured him—and avoided them carefully. Sometimes they were only mere eddies, curving ripples of tidal current, but he knew now how they were formed and found it no problem to get clear of them.

Long-stopping, as he thought it, was no longer ... difficult. At first much of it seemed strange. Until now, his life had been mostly in a quiet dark corner of a stinking ship, eating food with his fingers off something close to a wooden trough, fighting for each bite of greasy eel meat— which he had cooked—to keep it from the sailors who were also eating from the trough. He slept on moldy sailcloth jammed onto the rope in the rot-stinking anchor locker and wore clothing made from the same cloth. He had no real usable life then and if the boat stopped at some shore or port he was locked in the forward chain locker until they were at sea again. Always governed, held captive by men who seemed to own him.

But now he was alone.

Wonderfully, gloriously alone. And while it was tricky at first—getting free of unwanted company (bears), making a fire, some kind of shelter—he quickly came to enjoy it, then later love the freedom of it.

It took him almost no time to pull up the canoe, flip it over to make a lean-to shelter, find an abandoned mouse or squirrel nest to use for a fire starter, flick a spark, shelter it, nurse it into flame, and get a pot of soup going, made from dry salmon and grass, while he settled back on a rock to work on the story board, or make a spear, or to . . .

Just be.

It was as if the outside had become his inside. His place of life had gone from a dark little hovel in a half-rotten ship to all of everything. The forest, the sky, the water—all of it had become his home.

And he wondered, sitting by a drying fire when it was mist-raining, how in Odin's name could you carve that in a memory story?

Maybe there were some things you just had to live.

And so he did.

He worked north from inlet to inlet, stopping for breaks at islands that were free of bears until one afternoon—or morning, or evening, they all seemed the same in his new life—he pulled out of an inlet and started to paddle and noticed, felt, something different about the motion of the water beneath the canoe.

There was tidal movement still, as there always had been, currents he rode with or tied up to let go by, but something new.

There was a surge to it. A gentle rhythm that had nothing to do with the tidal currents. A new life to the water he had not felt beneath the canoe earlier that seemed somehow familiar. Seemed he should know it. Know the surge, the motion of the water.

And it came to him. It was the swells from the open sea. He had known it for years on the ships. Felt it for his whole life, though never in such close confines as it was now, caught in inlets and islands. Shaping, warping it.

The heartbeat of the ocean, Old Carl had called it. "Feel the pulse of it," he said, sitting one day on a pile of rotting rope, smoking the dis- gusting black tobacco in a small clay pipe that fit in a round hole worn in his teeth. "It's the pulse of the sea, going 'round the world. You might feel a swell that started days or even weeks ago, far away, moving without tiring, instead getting stronger the further it travels . . ."

And with the knowledge of the swells,

remembering them, he noted that the channel between the mainland and the big island had widened more and more as he paddled. Then, later, he saw the sun shining on an open sea. Saw the swells as they came marching in . . .

Different now. Everything changed quickly. Still inlets on the eastern side, and he could see more land in the distance ahead—days away— but he had gone from calm, lakelike waters among the islands to the edge of the immensity of the sea itself.

It was calm now, peaceful now, but not a place a canoe could live if the sea decided to become angry. He would be flipped, rolled, and sunk in moments if even moderate waves brewed up.

He would have to stay close, always close to shore, working in and out of the inlets so he could get to safety if the sea changed, came with added wind-force, at least until he had moved still farther north where there might be smaller islands and shelter from the open sea.

And there were new problems. As the sea grew larger it seemed his canoe grew smaller. Much smaller, in comparison with even the modest swells that came rolling in. A chip of wood, a leaf floating on a puddle.

Now the inlets became much larger and went back much, much farther. Immense, water-filled canyons with scores of waterfalls where small rivers dropped off cliffs so far the water sometimes turned to spray before it reached the surface. Nor were these canyons narrow slots, as so many inlets farther south had been. They could be very wide and this made everything more difficult.

If the canyon was deep, it might take him two or three days to go in and follow the shoreline around and back out. Traveling all that time to cover a distance that brought him only a short way farther north. Whereas if he went across the inlet at the mouth, he would not have to spend all that effort and time . . .

But again, the sea was big, his canoe small.

And the mouths of the inlets, because of their enormous size and depth, could become dangerous.

When the tide flooded in, countless amounts of seawater were pushed, jammed back and up into the inlet.

There would be a brief time when the tide was slack and the inlet was still. But that was followed by the deafening roar of the whitewater sea surging back out through the narrow mouth of the channel as the tide receded.

Leif was initially lucky because he came upon such an event while it was happening and tied to a tree ashore to watch it. He saw how powerful, how destructive it could be and knew he could never survive such an explosion of water.

So, he thought.

So he had choices. He could go back in and around all the inlets or . . . no. He had done one of the canyon inlets, all the way in and around, and it was all cliffs with no small islands for making a long stop; no shallow gravel beds to fish in. Just rock and cliffs and . . . no.

But, he reasoned, he could wait and dash across the mouth of the inlet when the tide was full and there was no current. Before the outward storm of water started. Just whip across.

And it worked.

The first time he tried it, he waited until the tide was full in, then dug deep and was across before the outward maelstrom occurred.

Slick, he thought—*slick as an eel.*

And again, the next inlet. And it worked again.

Which made him confident. *I can do this. It is just a matter of thinking it out.*

Then he came to an inlet which was twice as wide as the first two. Much more distance to cover. *But still*, he reasoned—*the same thing. Just paddle harder. Same thing.*

Only it wasn't.

He did it almost exactly right. Waited the tide out until it was full and the current seemed to stop and he set off.

But now there were several different elements that should have warned him—removed some of the cockiness from his thinking.

First, he found himself in close company with some new acquaintances. It was true he was now never totally alone. Ravens, and now seabirds, were always nearby, and he consistently saw orcas moving with him to the north. Most of them were at a distance and he was usually not close enough to see any distinctive markings. But killer whales were almost always in attendance.

But now, suddenly, he was surrounded by small dolphins. There were too many and they were moving here and there too rapidly for him to get a count. And they were not like the dolphins he had seen from the ships in the open sea. These were smaller, and colored much like the larger killer whales, with patterns of dark and light on their sides.

And very fast. They seemed to be toying with the canoe, rippling out in front of the small craft and down the sides, often so close Leif had to jerk his paddle out of the way to keep from hitting them.

They moved with and in the same direction as the canoe, sliding along with it, rolling now and then to look up at Leif, and he thought they seemed to be smiling at him, was pleased to have them in company.

And it was here he noted something else. Something not necessarily as pleasant. The water had changed. The tidal current was turning, was starting to move outward, which he had planned for and didn't concern him.

But.

Always that. But the swells coming in—not large, but consistent and very powerful in their movement—were flowing against the tide moving out and this created a crowning wave.

Small, at first. Just a nudge of water trying to curl over on itself.

But the swells kept coming in, pushing at the ebbing tidal current, and it kept trying to go out and the waves began to grow and Leif saw now why the dolphins were there.

They caught the wave, aimed nose-down in the same direction, and slid gently down and across the face of the great wall of water.

More, they were having a great time of it, rolling over one another on the face of the wave and for a few moments Leif smiled at their joyful games.

Until . . .

Until he realized he was moving with the dolphins. The waves were growing rapidly now as the outward flowing current gained speed and Leif felt himself—almost suddenly—losing control of the canoe as the wave grabbed and held the small craft.

The whole canoe was riding with the dolphins.

Only—quickly now—he found he was riding on the waves not with a sense of joy but of potential disaster. The growing waves were threatening to turn the canoe sideways and roll it.

He had to keep the nose in front, take the waves from the stern, keep the canoe from rolling and he dug deep with the paddle, one side and then the other, trying to increase the speed of the canoe and keep it ahead of the wave. Keep it aimed forward . . .

And failed. The wave was moving too fast, pushing the stern over to the side faster than he could keep it from happening. He was going to roll, felt sure of it, knew that if he did, the wave would just keep rolling the canoe, and him, keep him under the curl and drown him.

He thought for a part of a moment how silly that would be. To drown and die while riding with dolphins who were just having fun and with the thought came the knowledge that the answer was there.

The dolphins.

How did they do it? How did they keep from rolling in the wave?

He had moments. They were all around him

and he had just time for a quick look—a flashing moment of study to save his life.

And he saw it.

They didn't try to beat the wave. Didn't fight it. Instead they used their flukes and the curve of their bodies to aim themselves down the face of the wave.

Leif didn't have to fight the wave, compete with it. Instead, all he need do was use the paddle over the stern as a rudder, pushing sideways against the force of the wave to keep the canoe aimed down-wave, sliding with the wave, not fighting its force.

With the wave.

Of the wave.

Of the sea.

The canoe seemed to jump, come alive, as the stern answered and came over to the rear. The change was so quick it took his breath away. Exhilarating, even wild as the waves grew in size when the outward current flow became stronger still. He laughed out loud at the joy of it.

He quickly found that the canoe performed better not by going straight down the face of the wave but quartering forward, aimed off at a slight angle and—he saw the dolphins were doing the same thing—an endless, glorious slide-ride.

Except that it wasn't quite endless. *As nothing,* he thought, *is ever endless.*

Two things were happening that changed everything. The wave, with a curling white froth at the top as it bowed over, made a sound now, a threatening sound. As the wave gathered speed, the canoe tore down into the inlet, out of Leif's control, or nearly so.

He fought to keep afloat.

But worse, potentially more dangerous, as the wave pushed him into the inlet at ever-increasing speed it also, at the same speed, was carrying him across the mouth of the inlet, riding sideways as well as forward on the surface of the wave.

He was halfway across. Absolutely screaming along and, clearly visible now, at the other side the waves ran at an angle into the flat rock face of a cliff. And again, for that moment, there was nothing he could do. If he tried to turn down the face of the wave, it would roll him up and drown him and if he just kept riding the wave—which in his mind he now thought of as The Damn Thing—it would smash him into the rock face. Tear both Leif and the canoe apart on the rock with all the force of the wave. Nothing but pieces . . .

Nothing, he thought.

Nothing to do.

And again, at the most critical moment, the dolphins saved him.

Clearly they had done this many times, done it for fun, so they must know what to do and Leif watched them. Rolling, weaving over one another, looking up at him now and then, riding next to him in the wave, and as they approached the end of the ride—drawing close to the rock face—they simply peeled out of the wave and went to the rear. Some of them dove beneath the wave to get free, but most of them turned quickly around, so they faced the wave head-on, and slipped back over the top of it to the still water in back of the wave.

Slick, he thought for the hundredth time, *as slick as eel puke.*

All he had to do was spin the canoe around fast, really fast, no-mistakes-fast, and ride it head-on over the top of the wave. And then face the next wave head-on again, ride over it, and the next, and the next and . . .

Nothing to it.

He hesitated, realizing suddenly that as he spun around, the canoe would be for that instant side-on to the wave and could be caught and rolled. And then a part of him grew calm and he relaxed. He knew it was out of his hands. He was closer to the cliff face, rushing toward it, and there simply wasn't any time for him to think on it.

He took a deep breath, braced his knees at the sides of the canoe, dug the paddle in with everything in his arms, his back, and felt the canoe answer him. It swung to the one side, the bow sweeping, hung for an eternal moment as he heard the top of the wave hissing at him and the canoe shuddered once, her whole length, and passed through it and he was over the top.

He steered head-on into the next wave, half felt the water spray back on his face and chest as the bow cut through it, and he had a moment in the still water between the waves and then went over the next one as well.

And the next.

And the next . . .

He worked against the waves, heading out the side for the mouth of the inlet, until the tidal current heading out slackened and stopped. Now he had only the swells to contend with, taking them gently on the nose, sliding up and over them until he cleared the mouth of the inlet and moved north.

To the next canyon that cut back into the land, larger still than what he had just finished. But he knew how to cross them now, big or small, and he set to surf this new one—as the dolphins returned and surfed next to him—and he thought that was the difference.

He was learning . . .

No, not just that. He was learning to learn; knowing more.

He was bigger?

No. Not that either. As he moved north, saw more, lived more, he knew one thing for certain. He was the smallest part of everything he passed through.

So he wasn't bigger.

But he was still *more* in some way.

Had grown so that he was truly different from the orphan boy in the ships and he knew, believed and *knew*, that he would never be that boy again. That nothing on Odin's earth could make him become that again.

He smiled now, sliding in with the small dolphins, and the smile turned to open laughter as he felt the canoe come alive and ride the wave. He would find where a river came out and take fish and make soup with salt water and lie back in the sun.

In sun and joy, he thought.

That's what was really different.

He had found joy.

Dancing Giants

And now the country changed.

As he had changed.

For a slogging period of days the whole business of inlets disappeared and he was forced to paddle directly northwest up a long channel. There were nearly no side places to long-stop and rest, and when he finally had to just flat quit in exhaustion all he had available were thick brush and stunted trees that grew out of the side of rock faces to tie the canoe off to hang and rest.

When this happened—not just for long stops or often more briefly to ride out tidal current changes—he would sleep in the canoe. He had fortunately before this long, driving passage taken time to stock up on seven good-size salmon that he smoked. He had learned, or perhaps remembered—he couldn't be sure—to rub the salmon with salt water before smoking it and found that it made the oily meat taste even better and somehow be more filling.

There were no berries on this run, which he missed, and nothing to break the monotony except the ravens, and sometimes seagulls, which would occasionally stop and perch on the end of the canoe to rest.

He found that he was glad of the company, but did not see any killer whales or dolphins, and was ready to chuck it all and head back to more open water and inlets. What if, he thought, it was all like this from here on north? Just rock walls and the long work of not really getting anywhere. It seemed at times that what he was doing was sitting in one place paddling while the water moved beneath him. When he grew really tired, the rock walls seemed to also be moving, just sliding past the canoe while the water moved beneath.

His body started talking to him. His arms said they wanted to stop this endless working north, his back agreed with his arms, while his stomach grumbled because it had no berries. And he told them all to shut up. But he was near his end, and perhaps would have stopped, except he remembered something that Old Carl had told him.

It had been at his twelfth-year time. Leif had come to a part of his life where he couldn't stand it any longer. He had been captive, had been sold and traded from ship to ship, had been mistreated and beaten and was done. He thought he would go to the edge of the ship and jump over the side and let the sharks have him. They always followed the ship waiting for garbage and that's what he felt he had come to be: garbage.

But Old Carl had stopped him.

"It might get better," the old man had told him, "or it might get worse. We never know what is coming. All we know is that it will change—and what if it's something good that you miss because you gave up? Remember, it's only the water around your boat that counts. Everything else is just spit."

And Leif smiled now, thinking on it. No matter how his arms ached—it was still better than his life had been on the ships.

So he kept going, another day, and one more sleep, and the next time he awakened, he sat up in the canoe and looked ahead into thick fog. It was not something new—fog—and he disliked it for the way it blocked his vision.

He began to paddle, pointing ahead northwest up into the narrow channel and felt the tidal current pick him up and carry him along. He could see almost nothing—barely visualized what was directly in front of the canoe—but he sensed a change in the water around him. Felt the channel widening and the current that was pushing him slack off with the water becoming more spread out.

He could hear the birds—squawking gulls, gurgling ravens, overhead—thinking they must be above the fog or (more wondering) would they fly in fog as thick as this? Could the fog be that shallow in depth?

And now he heard a new sound that made no sense at all.

Huge splashing.

As if something enormous was getting dropped or thrown down on the water.

Out there.

In the fog.

Where he couldn't see.

Sometimes it seemed close, or again very muffled as if farther off.

And then nothing for a time.

And more. Two, three times—explosions of water-sound—with no order or rhythm. Quiet, then whoosh-*bang*!

Again, then it was gone.

He had quit paddling but when the water-thunder (as he thought it) seemed to have stopped, he started up again and had gone a while in the fog, stroking evenly, straight ahead, trying to push his eyes through the gray blank wall in front of him . . .

When suddenly, as if passing through a thick veil, he came out of the fog.

He had just two moments to see what lay before him. He had come out into a large bay surrounded by islands and the mainland on the east so it made an enormous circle of calm water.

And it was filled, absolutely filled with whales. There were spouts everywhere, one after another, and whales—not just killer whales but true giants of the sea—leaping up into the air and falling back with a large thunder-crash of water.

Then, directly in front of the canoe, the very ocean seemed to swell, pushed up from beneath—and first the nose, then the whole front half of a giant gray whale exploded up, towering over the canoe and Leif, hung for an instant, then slammed down and over to the side in an explosion of water and noise that seemed to engulf the whole canoe.

If it had come down on me, we never would have come up.

Leif couldn't believe the canoe was still floating. The pressure wave from the falling whale plowed into the side of the small boat, drove it sideways, skidding on the water like a chip of wood. He had no control. Had the opposite of control because everything he tried to do turned out to be wrong.

In the thick fog, paddling as best he could in a straight line, without realizing it he had come well out into the bay. He had heard the jumping whales around him but had seen nothing and now . . .

Now he could see everything.

And what he saw came close to terrifying him. He was smack in the middle of what seemed to be an Odin-inspired gathering of true giants and he suddenly remembered Old Carl watching Little

Carl trying to keep up and getting brushed aside with men at work saying: "When oxen dance in the barnyard, mice hide in their holes."

And now Leif was the smallest of mice in a massive barnyard. In the fog he had propelled himself out into the very center of all that was happening—a frenzy of whales.

Of course he had seen killer whales, orcas, very close; had touched one, made eye contact, and had seen giant whales before—when he was captive on the ships—but always at a great distance. Vapor spouts far away, now and then a set of flukes when a whale dove, again, never close. A brief flash of something black and shiny and wet off in the distance and they were gone. They always seemed to be trying to avoid the ships, always dove deep or turned away.

Never like this. They weren't avoiding anything, couldn't care less about a boy in a canoe and he realized suddenly what they were doing.

They were being whales.

This was how they lived . . .

And if I live, he thought, *I will have gotten to see this.*

At the moment he wasn't quite sure he would be able to pull it off. The whales that were jumping—he had come to believe they were dancing—were mostly gray whales, and when they came up, apparently from the bottom somewhere to get a good run at it, they blew out of the water so hard it seemed as if they were trying to fly.

But of course they couldn't, had to come back down, and they just as apparently had not had a usable plan on anything but just the leap up. They fell back wherever, however, and Leif knew if he happened to be under one when it landed he would simply disappear.

The end.

The trick was he didn't know how to avoid the jumpers. Since they didn't seem to have any coherent idea—just jumped wherever they happened to get the urge, or so it seemed—it was impossible to try to paddle the canoe in such a way as to avoid them.

Leif thought the best plan he might have, since the whales didn't seem to have one, was just paddle in a straight line out of the center of the bay— the middle of the frenzy—trusting to luck that a whale wouldn't land on him, and get to shore, set up a camp, and watch.

And it might have worked.

Had a chance to work.

Except that the dancing gray whales were not the only whales in the bay. The whales attempting flight and falling back, except for the killer whales— which seemed to be sweeping back and forth everywhere as if they were hunting something—those grays were the smallest whales in the bay.

There were also humpbacks, whose backs curved when they dove so that often their flukes rarely showed, and blue whales, so huge they would make two or even three grays.

And all of them, the humpbacks and blues, seemed to blanket the bay in a roiling, heaving mass that made the surface come alive with their backs, and they did not come to play. They were there to, perhaps, settle differences—at least from what Leif could tell, as they rolled over and on one another—but even more they were in the bay to feed.

Which was where it became difficult, nearly impossible, for Leif to sustain any kind of sensible direction to paddle the canoe.

It was the way they fed that made things tricky. A blue whale—which was longer than any ship Leif had sailed upon—would dive straight down, swim in a tight circle emitting bubbles so that it generated a circular, tube-shaped bubble-container—similar to the bubble-wall the killer whales had made to corner salmon against the shore—then deftly dive again, curve tightly up, open its wide gaping mouth, and blow to the surface filling its mouth with seawater and any small fish or sea creatures unlucky enough to have been caught and trapped in the bubble-walled cage.

At the top of this feeding procedure the front end of the whale's mouth would jam out of the surface, and he would slam it shut and squeeze out all the water, which had been captured in his giant, pleated belly, in a spray through what appeared to be a thick fan of dark hair bristles, which let the water through but retained any food.

When he saw it for the first time, Leif thought it was a great way to eat. Take it all and spit out what you didn't want.

He had part of an instant to realize he and the entire canoe were sitting inside a surfacing ring of popping bubbles, when the water around him detonated and a huge head of a blue whale emerged, brutally plowing the canoe sideways, nearly rolling it, and he was covered with the water the whale expelled out into the air.

It was similar to when the killer whales were

feeding and ignored Leif. The blue whale could not have cared less for Leif and the canoe—did not even seem to consider them.

He was there to eat.

Period.

And from that point on, the canoe and Leif were simply something to get out of the way, and Leif became most definitely the mouse in a barnyard full of dancing oxen.

No matter what he did, no matter what direction he moved, it was wrong. He tried first—as soon as he regained control of his abilities and realized he had not been swallowed by the gigantic mouth that came up beneath him—to paddle away from the blue whale, which was now sinking away to get ready for another go at it.

Only to find that he was on top of another ring of bubbles and had to grab the sides of the canoe and use his knees to keep balanced to avoid being rolled up and over and out of the way.

Trying, and failing, to keep calm, he took to

the paddle once more and tried to maneuver away only to find himself yet again in the wrong place as a giant open mouth exploded up under him.

If I just keep working back and forth . . .

But no. Along with the whales that were bubble-fence feeding, more, many more, were just lining themselves horizontally on the surface and lunge-feeding, thrashing with their flukes along the top of the water with their mouths open.

And so it went. Cut one way, mouth up from the bottom, cut another way, slam sideways when a lunge-feeder caught him, spin, up from the bottom, lunge, scoot backward to another bubble-feeder. Back and forth, to and fro, spin and jerk until somehow he found himself flattened against the shore, hanging on desperately to a dead tree limb that stuck out from a rock, without having the slightest idea of how he and the canoe got there.

He was soaking wet—the canoe had a lot of

water sloshing back and forth in the bottom—his hair was hanging in his face and a good-size piece of unchewed smoked salmon was jammed in his mouth.

Somewhere along the wild ride, he must have felt hungry and grabbed a strip of meat—though he had no memory of doing it—and in the furor of trying to avoid wrecks with the whales had forgotten to chew and swallow it.

He did so now, swallowing it in chunks, and dug out the copper pot and bailed the canoe out, all without really thinking. In the bay, which lay before him, the whales were still at it—jumping and falling and bubble-feeding and lunge-feeding—so that the surface seemed to be boiling with them.

But he was now well free of them, and crawling along the shore, he came to a small inlet—really little more than a dent in the side of the shoreline—and turned in. There was a little circular pan of gravel and rock—he could see no bear scat—and he pulled up the canoe, turned it over to dry out, and made camp near a trickling brook that came out of the rock and forest above him.

All this took no time or thought. It was becoming nearly automatic for him—quick fire-circle of rocks, a mouse nest to make a spark to make a fire to make . . .

To make.

All of it without thinking. Wherever he was now became his home, was as familiar as if he had designed things for himself, had put this firewood just here, put this mouse nest just there . . .

Of course there were life surprises that were not always good.

Like a sickness that killed or a whirlpool to suck you down or a surprise of coming out of thick fog into a frenzy of jumping and feeding whales without a warning. But you faced those things as they came and either were successful or you went to Valhalla.

That simple.

You lived or you died.

And in between the two, if you kept your mind open and aware and listened and smelled and watched ...

In between you learned.

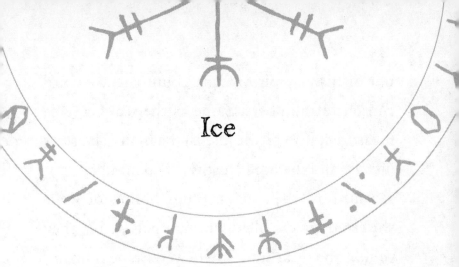

Ice

He now entered into an apparently end-less series of large bays with fewer small islands and only occasional forested inlets on the landward side.

A world of giants.

In his years of captivity on the ships, he had seen, known, many things that caused him to marvel. The ocean itself, the enormity of it, the way it never ended, never could end. He had been on deck one clear night sitting next to Old Carl and he looked up at all the stars and wondered aloud: "How many are there?"

Old Carl had laughed between puffs of smoke

out of his clay pipe. "Can't count them—you'd run out of numbers. Same as the sea. Can't be measured. Too big. It just is, that's all. The stars just are and the ocean just is . . . no numbers."

And now these bays. Huge bodies of well-sheltered waters filled with animals so big they couldn't be measured. There weren't, he thought, enough numbers. He had camped for three days on the side of the first bay, where he had been captured by the whales jumping and feeding, and then moved along the shore north. He kept close, almost touching the land, and for the most part the whales stayed out in the open water, though they were still active and provided him with a show whenever he stopped to camp and rest.

He had run out of salmon so he stopped at an inlet with a stream and spear-dragged ten good-size silvers that he smoked. This was not a safe island, and while there was no bear scat, he was concerned that the smell from the drying racks might bring bears so he slept light and had the canoe ready to push off into water in moments. But this time none came and to add with the salmon he found a good stand of berries and ate until his belly was tight.

It was here that he met with the ghost of his mother.

A huge gray whale came near the canoe and stayed by him when he stopped to sleep. He wasn't certain how he knew, but he felt somehow that it was a female and she, as he thought of her, stayed near him for days.

She was not aggressive nor even very active but several times nudged the side of the canoe when he was sitting in it and raised her nose to the top of the edge. He found himself smiling and then, without really knowing why, tried to picture-remember his mother and reached out to touch-pet the nose of the whale.

She came back time after time, floating next to the canoe and seemed very careful not to damage the boat or him, for she could have flipped the canoe over easily just by pressing down on the edge but didn't, and she seemed to enjoy his touch.

She was, he thought, kind. Somehow kind. She wanted to know him and he felt-thought a kindness from her, and every time they were close together he thought of his mother, how she must have been gentle this way, kind and gentle and caring and the whale made him deeply sad and in some way gently happy at the same time. Gave him a memory of something that never existed.

He named her Grace because he had known an old lady named Grace on the docks who took care of him and fed him by letting him suck on a milk-and-grease-soaked rag when he was an infant. She held him and hummed a soft sound when he was eating, a not-quite-music sound and he caught himself making the same sound when whale-Grace was nearby. A kind of not-song and not-chant while he daydreamed of how his mother must have looked.

Later he came upon a small island well offshore—they were more rare now in the big bays—and stopped for three days to dry clothing and the canoe a bit and whale-Grace left him. He mourned her leaving and for many days after that he kept looking for her as he paddled and stopped to rest, but she did not find him again.

All this time, out in the bays, the whale frenzy kept going. When he stopped to rest or dry out—it misted more often now—it was like a private show just for his entertainment. Once, when he was lying by a warming fire and watching out in the bay there were spouts of whales blowing everywhere, like little vapor trees growing and falling back and three times he saw two gray whales come up and out of the water next to each other at the same time, nearly touching, so that when they fell back they made a small mountain of a splash and he wondered if they weren't really dancing. Which made him wonder if they had music—he had heard their songs through the hull of the canoe when they were close—and if that might lead them to dance.

Big dance, he thought.

The biggest dance of all. Whale dance.

Everything now was bigger.

True mountains with snow-capped peaks could be seen off in the distance and the inlets—not nearly as numerous as they had once been—went far, far back in some places, endless. Literally mountain canyons filled with the sea.

One in particular he was interested in entering, could see that it went far back in a deep canyon, but the entry opening was too narrow and filled with such a ripping current he decided the risk was too great.

He had started to nose in but the water pummeling out simply flip-turned the canoe—he barely kept his balance—and shot it into the bay fast enough that he knew if he had become caught in it he would have been rolled up and sunk.

Learning. He was learning.

Some things he could do—some not. There was some comfort in knowing what he could do, what he couldn't. But a danger as well—if he thought he knew too much, knew everything—he could get in trouble.

The bays were now becoming so enormous they amounted nearly to open sea and if the wind came up, the surface went quickly to waves. Not the monster waves of the open ocean, where swells added to wave height, but still waves that could be as tall as he was if he were standing, and they seemed even taller as he knelt and paddled at the back of his canoe. Big enough to cause trouble for the canoe and Leif found that he could just weather them—pulling hard on the paddle—if he kept the nose of the canoe straight up into them.

Except they might push him backward while he was keeping the canoe straight and all the waves—or nearly all of them, depending on wind strength—blew directly into the shore. Without an inlet to hide in and do a long stop he became vulnerable to getting piled into the rocky shoreline and one good-size wave taking the canoe into rocks would crush the canoe and turn it into kindling.

And there weren't many inlets to hide in.

Which led more than once to Leif getting caught out in the open where he had to paddle—sometimes for full days at a time—to keep from getting, as he thought it, mushed on the rocks.

When this happened, and he was forced into paddling hard for whole days, he went beyond exhaustion, beyond even pain, and into a state of almost mental blankness. His body became little more than a paddling machine and his thoughts sought, it seemed on their own, for safety, of thinking, memories that would take at least his spirit to some other place while his body kept the canoe moving against the waves.

He thought of Old Carl, would think of how

he looked exactly, sitting on a coil of rope on the ship, or by a fire in the fish camp, one eye squinted because he was going blind in that eye and didn't use it much. Telling stories around his pipe smoke, head held tipped to the side; stories of sea monsters and beautiful women and things not always beautiful but always something to remember . . .

Now.

To remember when your body was beyond all things real, sensible, endurable, and had to endure just the same.

Or he thought of Little Carl and how he was always smiling . . .

Or he thought of how his mother must have looked, dream-memories still, though he had never quite seen her face in his dreams. Could never get her to turn her head just that little extra bit so he could see her . . .

Know her.

And it was in one of these all-day-driving slogs—as he thought it—against slamming wave action that he went past exhaustion and into a state that had him seeing hallucinations.

Whale spouts that weren't there . . .

Shimmering lights across the gray waters of the bay . . .

Clouds on the horizon in the shapes of buildings or monsters . . .

And, finally . . .

A blue ship.

He shook his head. The spray of the water hitting the bow of the canoe had constantly come back in his face and the salt in the water made his eyes burn and he wiped them, shook his head again, and tried to focus. For just that fraction of a moment he stopped paddling and nearly lost the canoe, had to jerk his body back to work and keep paddling before the waves turned him and rolled them up.

Look again. Stare into the distance. It was far off, but it was still there. Nestled on the far horizon, tucked neatly down in the mirror-mirage-light that shot across the waters, sat what appeared to be a bright blue ship with oddly misshapen white sails above it.

No.

No, it couldn't be a ship, and no, if it is a ship I want nothing to do with it, and no, if it is a ship it might be there to hunt the whales . . .

The big family of whales. My family . . .

And he didn't want them harmed. Taken. Killed. Melted down for oil. He knew that there were whalers, men that stank of burned flesh and grease—Old Carl said whale ships smelled as if they were made of rotten gut coils—worse than the dark ship that had brought death. And there was also that: This might be another ship of sickness . . .

So no. For so many reasons he didn't want it to be a ship, and in the same moment, he thought, how could it be a ship? Who paints a ship blue?

But if it somehow was a ship, he didn't want them to see him, wanted nothing to do with them, and he allowed the waves to push him slightly in closer to shore where he could not be easily seen against the rocks and forest.

He thought briefly of turning around and fleeing south, back down into the country of small islands and many inlets, but it was only a thought and his body kept paddling the canoe along the bank, north, toward the blue ship, pushed by some reflexive and instinctive curiosity that kept him moving, kept him wanting to know more.

To learn?

Did that have to enter into everything that happened to him?

So there it was: to learn.

He kept paddling and because nature had a way of doing things by itself the wind died down, which caused the wave action to quickly subside and an errant tidal current to come in, circling close to the shore heading in the same direction he'd been paddling so that in a very short time he'd gotten closer to the blue ship.

Which he saw more clearly now and could tell that it wasn't moving. It's true that the sails looked irregular, didn't somehow seem right, but still, the ship should be moving, and Leif paused, drifted with the current and wished Old Carl had added the small brass telescope he always had at hand to the pack he'd thrown in the canoe.

It was still far away, but now Leif could see that it didn't look like a ship—although it didn't look like anything else Leif could visualize either. It was huge, a big blue . . . thing. Some kind of giant blue thing floating in the water with white, glaring white peaks rising up in the air out of the top.

Closer still, he could see small, dark figures on the side, showing where the blue turned to white and as he watched, some of them slid off into the water.

Too small to be men. Short. Children? Children jumping off the side of the ship into the water? Cold, frigidly cold water?

No.

So, all right, he thought, trying to bring in some logic. It can't be a bunch of small children jumping into the water and really, closer still now, pushed by the current along the shore, he could see that it wasn't a ship, either.

And still closer and, finally, close enough to see what it truly turned out to be.

Blue ice.

It was something close to a mountain of blue ice, as blue as the sky, with white portions that hadn't turned blue, and there were seals all over the sides, some sliding off into the water and others exploding out of the water back up onto the ice.

He had heard of icebergs—the men on the ships talked of them, always in fear because they worried that the ship would run up on one in the darkness and be crushed and sunk. Old Carl said he had once seen a Greenland bear, white as snow on a piece of ice and that there were ancient songs about ice maidens that called men to their doom on the dark nights if they went to sleep on watch.

So Leif had heard of them, though not much that was good, and none of the stories he heard had talked of ice being blue.

Yet here it lay. Close now—he paddled closer to the side and even right next to the monster of ice—it still shone blue, bright blue, and when he found a small piece broken off and floating nearby he picked it up and saw that the color was all through it. He smelled the ice, tasted it, and found it was not salt, not frozen sea, but fresh water.

Which made no sense at all.

Here he sat, out in the middle, or nearly the middle, of a huge bay of salty seawater and this blue ice was as pure as if it had come from a fresh water spring.

No sense.

Close now, he paddled out around the ice— like going around an ice hill—and on the east side he saw a large inlet's opening, heading east out of the bay, and in the opening there was more ice. Smaller, but still blue and large enough to make him even more curious. He paddled toward that new piece of ice and looking back into the inlet he saw more pieces—some smaller, one large one—heading back to the east until he could not see more because there was a bend in the inlet.

It was, he thought, like touching the fin on the killer whale. The ice seemed to be leading him on into the inlet—how could he not go?

And so he did. There was a tidal current heading into the opening and he let it take the canoe. It wasn't fast—he saw that smaller pieces of the ice were drifting along with him, moving into the inlet—but it moved steadily along past intermittent sides of sheer cliffs and sometimes forested shores.

For a long time. Then the tidal current, which had been on the flood, turned and started out. Again, moving very slow, but enough to check his—and the ice's—inward movement. Rather than paddle against it, and not wanting to head back out, he tied off to some brush along the shore and waited it out.

Back and forth, moving with the current, then holding—as he had learned to do when he initially started north so long ago? He wasn't sure how long it had been, how far he had come.

The ice chunks, small and large, though, again, not as big as the first one he'd seen, were more and more frequent. The inlet was very wide, an enormous body of water, which must have been the reason it moved so slowly. He saw several pods of killer whales, not close enough to recognize any of them, but no larger whales and twice saw huge brown bears, working streams along the shore for salmon.

And it came to him, after a full day, that this inlet—really a fjord, as Old Carl would have put it—might go on forever. Tie into another ocean. Never end. And he was thinking of turning and going back the way he'd come when the inlet made a sharp turn to the side and he could see nothing straight ahead.

At that moment he heard something he thought was thunder. Muffled thunder and a crescendo of sound ricocheting along the walls of the fjord. So heavy a sound it made him stop and he thought it must be several gray whales jumping and falling back.

Before he could think much past the sound, a wave—head high—came barreling out of the arm of the fjord off to the side and nearly swamped the canoe. He just had time to swear an oath he had learned from Old Carl and grab a limb sticking out from shore while the wave passed under him flipping him up and back down . . .

Then nothing.

Not even the sounds of birds, which he thought were constant.

He waited.

It was like the thunder-wave—he considered the whole event as one thing—had deadened all sound and he sat, caught himself holding his breath, listening, waiting.

Nothing.

So he started paddling again. Reach ahead, pull

water back, reach ahead, pull water back until, at last, he came to where the fjord curved sharply to the west, rounded the corner, and found himself, he thought, felt, imagined to have come into a magical place.

The fjord ended in a small, almost perfectly round bay, and terminated in an enormous blue-ice wall. It towered over the circular bay. It was, he thought, as if the whole world had turned to ice. Light coming from the sun shone down through the blue ice, sprayed color-light across the water. Directly in front of him, between the canoe and the ice wall, was a large piece of ice that had clearly fallen off the wall; had made the thunder-wave that nearly swamped him. It wasn't as big as the piece out in front of the inlet that he had thought was a ship, but it was still huge, and the blue light coming from the sun and through the giant wall fought its way through this floating piece of ice and seemed to make it come alive.

Dancing light.

"Oooh," he said involuntarily. "What a thing"—the sound coming out as a whisper—"to see. What a thing it is to see."

The light seemed to come into, through him. He swore he could feel it, would swear all his life that he had felt the light in his body, shining through him, and he sat for a time he would not measure, dancing with light, wanting to sing with light, wanted his spirit to be the light. To be light.

Then, as if everything had been holding, waiting for him, he was besieged with the sudden noise of seabirds and the crack-splash as another chunk of ice—smaller now, but enough to make sound—fell off the wall. It made a wave as it hit the water of the bay and Leif saw the wave come out around both sides of the large piece of ice floating in the middle of the bay and close in on him.

He braced his knees and held the side of the canoe to stabilize it but the wave was fairly small and did not pose a danger.

But if a bigger wave were started . . .

This is not a safe place.

And the thought made him smile. There'd been lots of places that were not what anyone could call absolutely safe. All his life, he thought, his smile widening, had not been a safe place.

Still. Sitting in the middle of the fjord opening exposed him and what if a huge piece of ice broke loose, like the one the size of a ship? What kind of wave would that make?

He thought of Old Carl suddenly, talking of the sea and boats. "The ocean is so big," Old Carl had said, almost in a singsong, "and my boat is so small . . ."

The prudent thing, he knew, was to leave and head back out of the fjord. That was the safe thing to do.

And yet.

And yet he wanted to stay awhile in this place, this place of beautiful magic and blue light that danced around and through him and he found a small depression, a dip really, in the shoreline well off to the side away from the ice wall. Wasting no time—he did not want to get caught in the open if a large section of the ice wall fell—he worked the canoe up into this small cove and tied off to a small tree that stuck out over the water and stepped ashore on the rocks.

There weren't many small bushes—he guessed that they had been scoured out by moving ice— but he saw a single patch of blackberries and marveled at how they seemed to be in every possible place. He picked them clean and ate them with cold salmon and then sat.

Just sat on the shore and absorbed the ice wall, the grandeur of the place—it seemed like a giant theater with the sound of birds and moving water circling around and above in the swirling shafts of light and he thought that even with all its beauty this was not a place to live. To spend time.

No firewood, really. Just rocks. And while he

had passed some streams coming into the fjord they did not have shore-beaches, even stands of gravel and small rocks, but were mostly waterfalls or springs. Not useful places to set up a camp.

So he would leave this place. As he had left others. He would take slow pleasure and ride the tidal currents out of the fjord, back out into the bay of whales and move north again.

But for now . . .

Just for this, his own personal now, just for this bit of time, he would be in this place, of this place and take the beauty of this place into him.

Just for now . . .

And, maybe, the dream . . .

Dream Story

His trip north had become a movement through worlds. Some of them were harsh, even deadly, and some of them were gentle, even beautiful. He now moved into a time that he knew he would remember for the rest of his life.

After a few days he left the ice wall—timing his departure to leave just after a large piece fell off into the sea—and moved fast, paddling, digging into the water hard to move quickly with the outward-flowing tidal current to get well clear of any pressure waves that might follow another thunder-drop of ice.

None came and the weather, which had varied

between misty rains and sometimes—often—thick fogs, turned spectacular. The sun shone clearly day after long day, drying everything out, warming Leif down into his bones and he sat without paddling for long periods, just riding the flowing water, working on his story board while the canoe drifted with the current.

He chanced upon a small gravel beach with a stream flowing across it and there was dead wood for a fire so he stopped. There was no bear scat—now the first thing he looked for at any stop—so he set up camp, took ten salmon out of the stream, and set to smoking meat.

Again, it was like he had come home. All of it seemed as home, and with the fire and smoking meat racks and berries that he found it was a home with comforts.

He made hot stew with fish heads and skeletons, flavored with a bit of salt water, and relaxed into periods of deep sleep. The sleep was timed—along with ravens he was now followed by truly brazen gulls—so he awakened in spots to keep the smoke going, but when he went down, into it, he slept hard.

And dreamed . . .

And it was here, in this long period of rest and deep sleep, that he came to understand why he was doing the story board.

At first it hadn't been clear. He kept working on it, showing things that had happened to him, things he had seen and—trying in a picture— things he had heard, but he still wasn't quite sure why it became so important to him to keep a record.

Yet it was, it had become vital in some way he didn't quite understand. And so he kept at it, carving on the board when he had time, waiting for the current to change, sitting by a smoke fire, even drifting along in the canoe.

At the same time he had an active dream life. He had always dreamed a great deal, mostly scrambled thoughts, dreams that made no particular sense. But now and then, ever since he was a small child on the docks and on the ships, he would have the dream about his mother.

She had passed when he was born and so in some way he did not remember, nor think, that he had seen her. But he knew her, knew of her, had been part of her and so in some way could know of her, feel her, know that part of himself was from her, was in him.

Except in the dreams he could never see her face. She would be talking to other people— although he couldn't hear her voice except for a muffled sound—but always her back would be to Leif.

The dreams felt real. So real that when he had them he would awaken thinking he was with her and would somehow be able, awake, to move to see her face and would nearly stand up looking for her.

He thought she would be smiling.

He did not understand why he felt that—felt

her smiling—but would come out of each dream thinking if he had seen her, had been able to speak to her, she would be smiling.

She would smile at him. For him. It would be a gentle smile. A warm smile with kind eyes.

And this is how the story board happened, how it became not a story board but a dream board.

Because, he reasoned, if the dreams could seem so real, make him feel his mother was real, then they were indeed real. There was a dream world, had to be a dream world. And if those dreams from the dream world could come into his waking life, even for a moment when he first awakened, it stood to reason . . .

Stood to reason . . .

Stood to reason that he could take his awakened life, his open life, back into the dream world. If it could go one way, he thought, it could go another.

These are thoughts he had when he first

started going north, what he came to call The Long Paddle and for a time—having been delirious and hallucinating when he was sick—for a time he thought he was sinking back into that state, thinking that way about the dream world.

But then he thought when somebody was delirious, seeing things, imagining things, like dock people who had pickled their brains on ale and mead, they wouldn't know it.

So if he knew, or thought he knew, he was losing control of his thoughts, his mind, then it was sensible, a strange logic to think he wasn't delirious at all.

He was just Leif.

And if he wasn't hallucinating, there was a chance he was right. That some sort of dream world existed. And if there was such a place Leif might be able to gain entry into it.

He knew, or thought he knew, that he couldn't really go there, go into that world, even if it seemed real when he first awakened. But it was there, or he considered it to be actually there, and there might be a way to get information to that place.

To his dream mother.

And as he drifted north, riding the ocean's drift, he chewed on the idea until he at last came up with a solution, or what he thought might be a solution.

He would make the story board current, or as current as possible, and then each time he went to sleep—not dozing but a proper night's sleep—he would look at the story board so it would be the last thing he saw before he fell asleep. If he could bring the board into his dream, maybe he could work it around, while still in the dream, so even though he could not see his mother's face and smile and kind eyes, she might be able to see the story board.

And know of him.

And maybe someday, if he did it often enough, and succeeded, she would turn and he would see her face in his dream.

And because of all this, all his thinking and wondering, the story board became still more important and he worked on it, perfected it, sanded it with shore sand and shined it with fish oil until it looked like beautifully burnished old leather.

There was a small part of him that didn't really believe it would work, but a larger part knew he had to keep trying and so he worked on the board every chance he could, going back to recurve and reshape portions that he felt needed improving . . .

All this while working north, up along the shore, staying close, he became so intent on paddling and drifting and working on the story board that he was not immediately aware that the ocean, the sea, was changing.

What had been relatively small bays, play areas for whales, began to open wider and wider, until he began to feel the swells, the open sea giants that Old Carl said came from storms on the other side of the world, and when he looked ahead, way ahead, it was open ocean.

Big ocean.

And his boat was so small.

Still, he hated to be stopped and he thought at first that he could continue to creep along the shore, pulling up on land if the waves became difficult, continuing north. But as the swells grew only a bit larger the waves seemed to grab at the canoe, tossing it back and forth, and he found himself considering heading back south to where it was more sheltered.

And then he found the oar.

It was a full-on, long, two-handed oar, made of straight-grain spruce, no knots, and symbols he didn't know—OSPREY—were burned into the side of the shaft.

Leif snaked it out of the water along the shore and drifted while he looked at it more closely. It was clearly off a boat that had belonged to a ship, maybe a grease boat, perhaps a whaler, and with currents and swells and wind-drift it might have come from anywhere. Worlds away, across the sea ...

Except.

It had no weed growing on it, looked fresh and clean and virtually new, was the same color as clean honey—yellow-gold—enough to make him salivate. Plus it had not been eaten—there were worms in the sea that rapidly ate bare wood.

So it had not been in the water long. Not even weeks, maybe days, looking so fresh Leif found himself staring ahead, thinking he might see a ship, just there, just over the horizon.

With men.

A ship, men, a world he did not want to see, to face.

There might come a day when he would have to be with that world again.

But not yet.

I am not ready for that yet.

Not quite yet.

And he slid the oar into the canoe—might have use for the wood later—whipped the canoe around and headed south, breeze and current at his back.

Headed south down into that country where the ships would not come. Find a safe island up some big inlet and make a long-camp, even a winter camp. Make a bark hut around a fire-pit. Smoke winter salmon and hook-take some of those big flat bottom-fish with the clear meat Old Carl had talked about all the time.

Learn more.

Work on the dream and seeing his mother's face.

Might come out and cut north some sunny day when everything was right and see those ship people again.

But not yet.

He dug the paddle deep, felt the bow raise and slip through the water, nosing south.

Author's Note

I've been working on this story a long time. All my life, really.

When I was very young, just three or four, I lived for a short while in a trailer made of freshly sawn rough pine with my grandmother, when she worked at a cook camp for a road-building crew in northern Minnesota. There came a time at the end of each day when all her work was done and we would sit on her bunk, wrapped in a blanket, and count the mice that came out in droves after dark. I would drink a half cup of evaporated milk mixed with water (which I never learned to like) and would often eat a narrow slice of apple pie with sugar sprinkled on the crust (which I learned to love).

Grandmother would sip a cup of tea and when I had drunk my milk and eaten my pie and wiped the sticky off my fingers she would tuck the blanket tight around us, take a deep breath, put her mouth near my ear, and in a whisper that was almost a song, tell the stories.

No. The Stories.

She was from the Old Country. Norway. And in Norway she said you are either of the land or of the sea and much, perhaps all of her knowledge, all that she heard or was told in her stories, from her childhood, was of the sea.

Not silly fairy tales, these, my grandmother didn't read me nursery rhymes; she told unforgettable stories of the sea, so real I could smell the salt and hear the creaking of rope and wood and picture North Sea waves so huge they raged far overhead and turned longboats into warping wooden sleds as they raced down the roaring-boiling face of water.

Grandmother wove her sea stories into my thoughts each night in the cook camp until I went to sleep dreaming the tastes and smells of salt herring and dried cod so deeply that the rich stink-taste was there the next morning when I awakened.

She brought the sea that was in me, out of me. Forever.

Locked.

So that when I was seven years old and crossed the Pacific Ocean with my mother in an old troop ship to be with my father in the Philippine Islands and came on deck to see the ocean, to see-smell-feel the open sea out around me like an intense deep-blue bowl, I was immediately, completely, overwhelmingly taken by it. I felt it calling, as if it were of me, in me, and I think it was very directly a kind of love, though I didn't think of such things then, just felt them. For several held breaths I didn't—couldn't—think of anything. Just that blue bowl going up into the sky.

I felt like I had come home.

And it would never leave me. Driven by some sort of genetic blood-memory, fueled by my grandmother's stories in the cook camp, all the rest of my life if I wasn't near or on the oceans I missed them. Became caught in a kind of homesickness. Then.

Almost exactly twenty years later, when I was twenty-seven and had done with the army and was trying to learn to write, a dear friend took me up to her parents' lakeside house at Lake Arrowhead, California. It was a beautiful spot with a wooden dock that went out from the shore, and tied to the dock was a small sailboat. It was old, tired, made of coarse plywood, and sloppily painted, but it had a mast and a single sail. The sail was raggedly tied around the boom and drooping into the boat, which had three or four inches of dirty water sloshing back and forth on the bottom.

All in all, not a pretty boat and not one I would have looked at twice. I knew nothing of sailing then—less than nothing. I had gone across the Pacific Ocean in a ship, powered by engines. Why would I care about something as archaic as sailing?

And yet.

And yet.

When my friend asked me if I'd like to try sailing I thought, truly, *Why not?* So she set me to bailing with an old coffee can while she pulled up the sail and cleated off the halyard and pushed down a flat board that went through a housing in the boat and into the water—a center-board, I would learn—that kept us from sliding sideways across the water. She then put the rudder down on the stern, handed me the tiller, untied the line that held us to the dock, and pushed off.

There was only a slight breeze but it caught the sail, pushed at it while she sheeted it in, told me how to handle the tiller to make the boat steer in the right direction, and off we went.

Moving.

Sailing.

I remember the feeling when the sail caught air and the boat started moving. As if it suddenly came alive, transformed into something else, some wonderful thing rather than a neglected tub of moldy plywood and ragged sailcloth.

It danced.

And I was to be irrevocably hooked on that dance for the rest of my life.

As I had been with the sea.

So I suppose it was inevitable that I would ultimately bring sailing and my love of the sea together—as natural as breathing—and it started me in on a seemingly endless procession of boats and what could be called passages.

In small boats—never much over thirty feet, good boats, some not so good, and some downright bad—I threw myself at the ocean and wind. Starting in Ventura, California, I sailed south down Baja and up into the Sea of Cortez, across to Puerto Vallarta, back to the Pacific side of Baja, north to California, and then across to Hawaii, down to Samoa, Tonga, over to Fiji, back up to Hawaii to sail the whole chain of the Hawaiian Islands, and across to California—sometimes alone, more often with friends for crew.

I learned to sail. To be part of wind and sea and wave.

Finally, back once more in Ventura, California, I outfitted a boat that was all I could afford, a boat so clunky and poorly designed, such a poor sailor, that I heard others call the make "an ocean-sailing turd."

North.

That was my plan. To sail the entire west coast of North America.

Slamming, always slamming, against appalling wind and waves around places of often blinding horror like Point Conception and Cape Mendocino off California, Cape Blanco on the coast of Oregon.

Slamming, always slamming until steering at last in the Straits of Juan de Fuca, first east and then north and the tidal rips—oh my god, for the tide rips—up to the north end of Vancouver Island. Then heading into the open, savagely open, north Pacific, where the storms come down from the Bering Straits and where the sea and wind and sky and thick fog are all working together, trying to kill you.

Big whales, which either ignored me and went about their lives, feeding and singing and dancing, or if they paid attention to me personally were, to a whale, friendly and open. Gray whales in particular seemed to like to be, literally, in touch with people and often raised their nose up onto the side of the boat to be touched, petted. Even blue whales, which are truly enormous—the largest animal that has ever lived on the planet, larger even than giant dinosaurs—would often stay close and allow touching, although I never had one deliberately put its nose up on the side of the boat.

Orcas, also known as killer whales, reminded me of wolves—in a positive way. Those that I saw, even when I accidentally intruded on their life while they were feeding or mistakenly got between elders and their young, were not particularly aggressive or threatening, just businesslike about solving the problem: moving me away or isolating me.

Once, in the middle of the night in bad weather where the Columbia River comes slashing out to the sea, I had been caught up in dodging half-sunken logs pushed out of the river into open water—many boats have been sunk by them over the years—and I accidentally moved between what I found to be a large male orca and his family pod. He was well back, perhaps a quarter mile, and when he saw my boat nearer to his family than he was, he thrashed the waves with his flukes and roared up between us, jumping well clear of the water as he came next to me—all of him in midair—to show me that he wanted me to move away. Now. I did so and that was it; no further demonstration.

When I first saw an iceberg, near the entrance to the Tracy Arm Fjord, south of Juneau, it was from a distance of six or seven miles and I was certain it was a blue-and-white cruise ship. My boat was very slow and moved toward it in seeming inches. I noticed in time—still thinking it was a ship, not an iceberg—that it wasn't moving at all. Ships, to retain control, must keep moving and this one seemed locked in one place. So perhaps, I thought, either a ship in trouble or not a ship.

As I at last drew near enough to find it was a giant blue iceberg, I was absolutely stunned by its size and color. It was huge, like an ice island, and as blue as the sky. Blue icebergs are formed from older, deep glaciers whose massive weight, over an uncountable amount of time, compresses much of the air out of the snow and ice. The subsequent airless glacial ice becomes a beautiful blue and is eventually "calved" into the sea. It incidentally melts very slowly as well, as I found when chunks were put in the crude ice-box on my boat. The reason this berg was so still and unmoving was that as the tide moved out and the water became more shallow it hung up on the bottom. When the tide came in, the water grew deeper and it floated again. They are not particularly dangerous except that sometimes they are fairly top heavy and will roll-flop over suddenly. If you are caught under one, it will obviously go very bad—like having a small country land on you.

One evening I was tucked in a cove on the north end of Vancouver Island, a cove I heard the fishermen call Chickenshit Cove because they use it to hide from the astonishingly horrible storm seas to the north, where in the open ocean top-breaking waves of up to a hundred feet in height simply destroy.

Destroy.

I was tied off to trees on the bank, licking wounds and repairing broken bits of boat, while killer whales came to rest nearby. And as

I sat there drinking a cup of lukewarm tea that smelled of bilge water, resting half asleep, half in a kind of exhaustive coma, sleeping with eyes open, brain taking care of itself, this story . . .

Leif's story . . .

like a soul dancing on sweeping raven wings . . .

started to come into me.

The wild sea coast Leif covers is a mythical frontier, inspired by the North American coast I traveled as well as the Norwegian coast of my ancestors. For certain, vast distances have been traveled by wooden canoes. Indeed, canoes only slightly bigger than Leif's, connected in pairs side by side with cross poles tied down to make a crude catamaran, have crossed oceans.

Still, there were places on my own journey where Leif could simply not have gone; inlets with tidal currents so powerful it is nearly impossible to broach it and enter the fjord. One such place is named Ford's Terror Fjord, where I made it through and long-camped (as Leif would say).

It is stunningly beautiful once you are in, with waterfalls and rivers and salmon-fishing bear, but getting there would be tricky and potentially dangerous in something as slight as a dugout canoe.

Cholera is the disease that triggers Leif's journey—a common killer throughout history, and one that still affects up to four million people a year around the world. It is caused by fecal matter infected with the bacterium *Vibrio cholerae* getting into food or drinking water—a typical method of spreading is flies carrying it from waste to food or water—and it has a gestation-to-lethality period of between one or two hours to five days. It can lead to an awful death by diarrhea and vomiting, causing massive dehydration and total system shutdown, but today is preventable through vaccination and sanitary measures and curable by aggressive rehydration techniques and antibiotics.

The truth is, much of what Leif faced was because he was in "not a safe place," but then, as he put it, his whole life was not a safe place. But